PUFFIN BOOKS

BREAK IN THE SUN

When Patsy Bligh's mother remarries and has another baby, the whole family leaves its small, pretty home in Margate and moves to a block of flats in London. It's then that Patsy's troubles begin, for she hates her new home and her cruel and lazy stepfather. Soon Patsy's worries start to show themselves in an embarrassing and unexpected way – a way that leads to more rough treatment from her disapproving stepfather.

The only person that Patsy might confide in is her school friend Kenny, but he has enough problems of his own. All his life Kenny has been the fat one. Tubby, Porky, the boy that everyone else taunts and laughs at. So Patsy can't count on much help there. But just when things seem absolutely desperate, a chance of escape presents itself. There's a boat on the river carrying a group of actors down to the Kent coast for a few performances . . . and they need someone to take the part of a young girl. Will Patsy have the courage to go off? And how will her mother and stepfather react?

This is an absorbing story, for eleven-year-olds and over, of how one young girl copes with difficult circumstances in a dramatic and enterprising way.

BERNARD ASHLEY
Break in the Sun

Illustrated by Charles Keeping

PUFFIN BOOKS

Puffin Books, Penguin Books Ltd, Harmondsworth, Middlesex, England
Penguin Books, 625 Madison Avenue, New York, New York 10022, U.S.A.
Penguin Books Australia Ltd, Ringwood, Victoria, Australia
Penguin Books Canada Ltd, 2801 John Street, Markham, Ontario, Canada L3R 1B4
Penguin Books (N.Z.) Ltd, 182–190 Wairau Road, Auckland 10, New Zealand

First published by Oxford University Press 1980
Published in Puffin Books 1981
Reprinted 1981 (twice), 1982 (twice), 1983

Made and printed in Great Britain by
Richard Clay (The Chaucer Press) Ltd,
Bungay, Suffolk

Dedicated to my mother, Vera Ashley

I should like to thank Bob Cattell of the Greenwich 'Bookboat', and John Munson, for their help with matters relating to the *Dame Sybil*.

All the places mentioned in the book are real except for Steeple Stones, which is, however, very near Whitstable ...

I

Two people had secrets up on the roof of Riverside School. One was the caretaker, who knew his supervisor hated climbing stairs and was no way likely to see the unrepaired desks he'd stacked against the skylight. The other was Patsy Bligh, who whenever she went up there to take the temperature for the weather chart—one day in five—always took the time to stare out at the river, and to dream her secret dream.

It was a big secret, this dream: it was the whole of the broadening river as it drifted out of London, carrying her with it on one of the tides; a secret return to the past; a self-made promise which somehow kept her going. But, huge as it was, it still seemed too small to make up for everything that had happened.

Today was a good day, though. First, there was the weather. It didn't need a temperature reading to know it was hot: it had been scorching all morning, glorious sunshine without the whisp of a cloud. And on top of that, Patsy had had a run of a couple of good nights. She felt normal, like the others; and that was a rare treat. The class-room windows were open, and somewhere below the narrow veranda a bird sang between the rumbles of the lorries. Everyone was getting on with their topics, Mary McArthy had made her die laughing at break-time, and Mr Lamb had sent for a pad of merit slips. So at least some things were good.

And they needed to be: because since Eddie Green had come, things had changed at home, and now it was all very different for Patsy. It wasn't Patsy and her mum, upstairs in Mrs Broadley's little house any more; but Mr and Mrs Green, and Patsy, and the baby, Jason. And there were different rules in the flat. There were wet beds, too, and hard smacks for her own good, and him only ever saying her name like it was a swear-word. So school, when things were all right, was a good place to be, with its high view of the river and the regular chance for her to dream her special secret.

Mr Lamb finished shuffling through a pile of tear-off replies in a box file and he let the spring go. It surprised the quietened class-room.

'Well, yes,' he said into the sudden attention, 'now there are one or two of these I've not had back. Er, Patsy Bligh. . . .'

Patsy looked up from colouring a bright kingfisher she'd drawn, a traced bird with long legs added.

'I haven't had your permission slip, have I? The trip's only a week away now, straight after half-term. Did you take the letter home?'

Patsy nodded.

'Well, what did they say? Can you go? Because, we can't take you without permission, you know that. . . .' The young man smiled, and looked reasonable.

Patsy nodded again and pushed a tangle of fair hair off her face. How could she tell him what they'd really said—Eddie Green, the little hard-handed man who lived in his armchair, or Mum with her ratty headaches. 'I dunno,' she decided to say.

'But I must know, love. And it's Friday. Mrs Daulton wants it all done for this afternoon. Lester Drew, what about you?'

'Can't go.' Lester said it quickly. 'Can't afford it.'

Mr Lamb shut the box-file. 'Not to worry. I'll see you in a minute, Lester.' He turned back to the real problem. 'Now, Patsy, where do you live?'

She looked up from the kingfisher again. 'Twenty-four, Harding Court.'

'Well, that's not far,' he said. He glanced at his watch. 'It's nearly half-past twelve. Do you reckon you could nip home, and get your slip, and be back by one o'clock? Is anybody in?'

Oh, yes, Eddie Green was always in. Patsy nodded again, but it was hesitant now, like someone bidding for an expensive item at an auction.

'All right; well, look, you do that, and come straight back with it. Bring it to me in the staff room. All right?'

'Yeah.'

'Eh?'

'Yes, sir.' It was louder, but not confident: because she knew—as she'd known all along—that whatever face she put on it for Mr Lamb she'd only have all the trouble over again when she got home. Him in the armchair, strict and spiteful, pretending to her mum that it was all for her own good; and Mum standing there nodding to keep in with him.

'O.K., well, straight there and straight back. And report to me in the staff room. We must get this sorted today.' Then he smiled. 'Because you don't want to miss our history-mystery tour, do you, Patsy?'

'No, sir.' And she didn't, either. It sounded good, in a big school bus, going from place to place down in Kent. The only problem was likely to be the condition Eddie Green made for letting her go.

Once out of the school building the full warmth of the sunny morning hit her, and slowed her. The recent heat, like the comforting showers at swimming, made her want to do no more than just stand there and be warmed by it.

It was a day in a thousand: the sort other people always seemed ready for, with sun-tops and dark glasses. Along the shopping stretch the buses tacked on hot roads, and a telegraph pole was dripping black. Already, the drains were latticed with dusty cobwebs. But Patsy didn't go far along that way. She turned off between two shops and kicked along the dusty riverside walk, the pedestrian route to the flats, and she felt a slow pleasure take her over in the quiet, uncrowded heat.

This was a winding walk by the water, between the shopping centre and the estate, a path for the day-time only,

3

with a corrugated factory fence on the left, and the flat spread of the river on the right. It only amounted to a couple of hundred metres in its length, but being away from the road and busy people made it a bit like the country to Patsy, and she looked to where an edging of pale urban weeds seemed like a lane, and to where the brown river, sparkling darkly on the surface, drifted off to places where Eddie Green would never be. She found a cornflower, long-stalked and small-headed, wild and strong and pure blue. She picked it and stuck it through the cardigan they'd made her wear. That was pretty, wasn't it? Different from the others, she thought. Better than dandelions.

It had been a lot like this, once upon a time, in that little street in Margate. In the small house behind the amusement park, with the pretty front garden, and Mrs Broadley downstairs, there'd been so many flowers like this to pick, and always time to put them in water. That had been good; when the only times Mrs Broadley had thumped on the ceiling with her broom handle had been to call her down for cartoons on her colour television, and biscuits, and cups of sweet tea. But that was before Eddie Green: before the move to London: before Patsy's troubles had begun. And before she'd started dreaming of that river trip away, back down the Thames to Mrs Broadley who knew her, and who really understood. . . .

Meanwhile, the sun was still warm on her head, and she couldn't help feeling better for that. She skipped, one step in four or five—just an irregular lightness in her walk and a long way from dancing—and she began to feel more optimistic. He'd have to be all right about it, wouldn't he, after two good nights? She hadn't done it since Tuesday. Yeah, odds-on he'd sign the form for her. Please God let him sign the form. . . .

'That's pretty. That's pretty, little girl.'

Patsy stopped dead: off balance. Who the devil was that? She hadn't seen anyone along the path; there'd been no one in front, no one following behind. She swung round, but still she couldn't see anyone. It had been a stupid sort of voice, like someone taking the mickey, just the sort of thing the factory men did at times. Yeah, it was probably someone in the factory yard on the other side of the fence, she told herself.

There was a laugh.

'Down 'ere. Look, I'm down 'ere!'

Her eyes flashed to her feet. So he was, down on the river side of the path, just his head showing above the tops of the thick posts. So there was no danger from grabbing hands. A long, white face with reddish, watering eyes was held level with her legs as he clung there two metres above the mud. He was looking at Patsy as a toddler might stare at a sudden cat, and she wondered if it could be her party dress that was so pretty. She'd been wearing it for three days and it was creased, but it was shiny and pink.

'It's blue. Pretty blue.'

He couldn't point from where he was, but he nodded, and Patsy squinted down her front.

'Oh, me flower. Yeah, nice, in't it?' Soft in the head, she thought. One of the barmies who hung about in the day. But he'd be harmless; they all were. Mary McArthy ticked them off as if they were pet dogs, and ordered them about to make them laugh, and they never seemed to mind.

'What flower?'

He was leaning his arms along the parapet now, and wrinkling his face in pretended thought.

'I dunno.' Apart from dandelions she only knew daisies for sure. 'You tell me.'

The man shook his head slowly. 'Pretty.' And then with strong arms he was pulling himself up to sit on a post top, rubbing the green from his hands down his trousers.

They stared at one another, the man smiling, Patsy's face suddenly uncertain. Mary McArthy or one or two of the other kids were usually about when this sort of thing happened. But she was on her own now.

She worked out the possibilities. Which way would be best to run if she had to? Left, to the flats, or right, back to the

5

shops? Was she half-way along yet? She smiled at him, bravely, as she would at a dog she wasn't sure about.

Talk to him was best, she thought. He could grab her now, but he was soft, and she could easily fool him. Anyway, they were all harmless, these barmies, weren't they?

'What you been doing?' she asked. She tried a casual lean against the corrugated iron, squinting at him in the river glare. But she didn't relax: and she wouldn't half go quick when she went!

He patted the bulging pockets of his jacket. 'Been doing work,' he said. 'All old iron for Mr Greenslade.' With difficulty his big hands worked out a rusted pulley from one pocket, and a smooth, black pebble from the other. 'Mr Greenslade give me wages when I do my work. . . .'

Patsy forgot about being ready to run. He wasn't very old, this man; not nearly as old as Eddie Green; and he was smiling. He seemed pleased to be showing her his morning's work, especially the 'old iron' pebble.

'That's clever,' she said. 'Finding them things.' On an impulse she took the cornflower from her cardigan and held it out. 'Here,' she said, 'you can have it if you like.'

'Thank-you-very-much!' It was a childish snatch, with a wide grin.

''S all right. I was only gonna throw it away in a minute.' And that was true; because it was no good going into the flat looking as if she'd stopped to pick flowers on the way. It didn't pay to look happy.

With supreme concentration the man pushed the cornflower's wiry stem through the top buttonhole down his jacket, and then he sniffed it, loudly.

'Pretty.' His eyes stared down, an intense blue. At that moment nothing in the world existed but that flower.

Clear off now, thought Patsy, now he's happy: run home quick and see what they say. But before she could move a sudden splash surprised both of them: a watery explosion from somewhere behind the man, further out into the river where a line of posts went deep. It was a big splash—like a dog, or a body, or a belly-flop on purpose.

The man was on his feet, squinting. 'Boy swimming,' he said, sounding sulky at the competition for Patsy's attention. 'Silly fat boy drown.'

And now Patsy could see him: it was a fat boy all right; it was Kenny Granger from downstairs, doing a stylish overarm in an arc away from them, down river. He wouldn't drown, she thought, he was too good for that. He might get shouted at for swimming in his bare bum, or for bunking off from school again. But that was about all. With his mum he wouldn't get no smacks.

She sighed, and stood up off the fence. 'Well, ta-ta,' she said to the man. 'I've gotta hurry. . . .'

But the man was still being cross with the boy in the water. 'Silly boy!' he shouted. 'Silly boy got no sense!' And he twisted his face at the river.

Patsy went, while his mind was somewhere else. There was still a bit of a distance for her to go before the riverside path opened out on to the patch of bald grass by the flats. She'd better not waste too much time. Besides, she wanted to get this over with. She walked fast, deliberately ignoring her sharp noonday shadow, which intrigued her less than its long-. legged sister had the afternoon before. This wasn't the time for walking slowly home, moving tall and beautifully across the ground, flouncing the shadow gown that her dress became. She couldn't do it today, imagining herself on the TV commercial, taking drinks from a waiter's tray—or like the girl down there, lounging back in the sun, deciding what she'd do tomorrow, planning how to please herself.

The girl down there! Patsy stopped again. Here, this wasn't something in her head! This was real. The girl in the white bikini, and the drink, and the boat she was on—the deck shining gold with varnish, the sides a deep blue like velvet. And what a beautiful girl . . . and calling up to her. . . .

'Hello, young lady.' She was waving as if she was really

7

pleased to see Patsy, sitting up and hugging her knees. 'What a gorgeous day. . . .'

Patsy leant over the parapet.

'But I can't lie out too long. I'm glad you came by. Sunbathing's not really my scene. I only go red, and burn.' She pulled a towel over her knees and draped another round her shoulders. 'Come and talk to me. . . .'

Patsy wasn't sure. This was the second stranger she'd met in three minutes, and she had the nagging feeling that she'd already been lucky enough for one day.

On the other hand, you didn't often see a sight like this down in the creek; and there weren't many people she met who gave her such a welcome.

Two minutes, she'd give it, and keep her distance.

'Do you like Coke, with a chunk of ice in it? Silly question, who doesn't?'

'O.K., then. But I've only got a minute.'

'All right, coming up!' And the girl dropped her towels and shimmied across the shining deck to the small wheel-house. She went inside and disappeared below.

Patsy waited and tried to stop thinking out any consequences, beyond her just having the cold Coke and then definitely running straight home. Well, she could give it a few minutes. Eddie Green wouldn't know what time she'd left the school, so he couldn't say she'd dawdled. And the Coke would be nice—a change from tap water and school milk.

But, God, it was hot, standing there in the baking sun, she thought. She took off her cardigan, and hung it on a tough splinter of wood above the boat. Feeling cooled by the nearness of the water, she sat with her feet dangling half a metre above the deck.

A beautiful boat, this was. Nothing creaky and rotten, with holes in the boards, like most of the stuff that got washed up around here. It belonged in a film, or in the rich sort of dream you had where things didn't go all wrong. With a boat like this you expected to hear soft music, and see men with

8

sun tans in smart, white suits, offering round the cigarettes.

But this was real, all right. The girl's shoulders, when she came back under a wide hat, were definitely very red, and you could hear the fizz of real Coke as the glass was handed up.

'My name's Jenny,' the girl said. 'And what's yours?'

'Patsy.'

The girl smiled and widened her eyes in a special look. 'Hello, Patsy.' She swept her arm around the empty deck. 'The others have gone shopping. At least, I hope so. There are some shops over there?'

Patsy nodded. 'The High Street,' she said.

'God, I hate shops, unless they're piled high with good gear, of course. This dragging round Sainsbury's scene definitely isn't me. And I'll say that again. Cheers.'

The girl clinked an imaginary glass and the Coke fizzled cool in Patsy's mouth.

'So, are you on holiday, or something? I've not seen any other kids around.'

It was too complicated to explain, so Patsy nodded in her glass.

'I hated school. Couldn't wait to leave. It's all rubbish, this best-years-of-your-life stuff.'

Patsy burped. 'Pardon.' It wasn't school, she thought. It was being at home was the trouble. Lying about on a shining boat looked much nearer the mark.

'Do you live near here?'

'Up in them flats. Do you live on this boat?'

'No such luck. Just for the week, while we're touring. . . .'

Patsy frowned.

'We're a theatre group, lovey. Not professional, just for fun. But we've all taken the week—next week—and we're going off on the boat to do a little tour. . . .'

Patsy was still frowning. They had theatre groups come round the school, but they came with all their stuff in a van, not in a beautiful boat like this.

'. . . The man who lives on the boat knows people down on

the Kent coast, where he used to live. Theatre groups, like us. We do our play in their halls. Nice holiday, eh?'

Patsy nodded. Down the Kent coast sounded all right to her.

'It's a play. A comedy thriller. Where you laugh one minute and you're scared stiff the next: you know?'

Patsy smiled, enviously. It sounded O.K., a whole week away doing something like that.

'Anyway, I like it. No big part to worry about: I just have all the fun. Walking on and walking off, and getting a few laughs. You know what I mean?'

Yes, Patsy did. They sometimes did plays in the hall. It was good. She enjoyed being someone else for a change.

'I've done some of that,' she said.

'Really? Are you any good at it? I bet you are, because you seem a natural for Tracey. . . .'

'I'm all right.' She was quite good, she thought. She enjoyed being stroppy old women and awkward customers in shops.

Jenny took the glass back, while Patsy crunched the ice cube.

'It's a pity we're not doing it here. You could've been our Tracey.'

'Who's she?'

'Oh, she's the cleaning lady's daughter in the play—my daughter, actually.' The girl laughed at the thought. 'She comes in near the end of the first act and tells the police about a mysterious man she saw in the lane, just after the murder!' She rolled her eyes, dramatically. 'But the girl's got mumps, or measles, or something, so she can't come. We're getting round it, but it's not the same. It makes a good curtain, usually.' Jenny shook the glass upside down, and she went to turn away; perhaps thinking of going below to do some job.

'I'm on holiday,' Patsy burst out. 'Why don't I come with you and be this kid?' Her eyes were shining. She knew it was a crazy thing to say: there was no way she could ever do it: but

10

wouldn't it be great, going down to the coast on this boat, and doing acting?

Jenny's face clouded. 'Oh, we'd love you, sweetie, we really would. But we're going right down to Sheerness, and Steeple Stones, and Margate. We're away for the week. Oh, lordy, I wasn't serious, sweetheart. . . .'

All at once Patsy's mouth felt electric dry. Margate, did she say? Her Margate? As far as that? This was what she'd been dreaming about for the past two years, wasn't it? Margate, and Mrs Broadley. . . . Like someone deaf learning to talk she found it hard to form the words. It had suddenly become essential. 'But . . . I'm on holiday. All next week. . . .'

'Yes, lovey, but your mum wouldn't dream of it, not with a crowd of strangers. And there's all sorts of legal stuff, I'm sure: letters of permission and all that. Cut my tongue out, I shouldn't have said it, should I?' She pretended to look at a watch on her bare wrist. 'Look, lovey, I've got a mountain of lettuce to wash before the others get back. Honestly. So I must fly. But it was really great meeting you, er—'

'Patsy.'

'Of course; Patsy. Well, 'bye, sweetheart, mind how you go now. . . .'

Moving fast, the girl got to the wheel-house and disappeared, with just one last wave of her wide hat: while Patsy, feeling the real physical pain of disappointment—the worse because it had suddenly all seemed so possible—turned away from the shining boat and walked on slowly towards the tower block.

Without any other disappointment to bring her down, just waiting at the door of the flat was a depressing experience. The sounds coming from inside were never the sort to lift anyone; there was no music station playing, no sudden whoop or burst of laughter; all you could ever hear was Jason whining or Eddie Green complaining. Patsy's was a place for going from rather than coming to.

She rattled the letter-box and looked through. Of course

they were all in, they always were. They'd never dream of going out to one of the parks to make the best of the weather; not them. They'd rather stick inside. She could see Eddie Green's socked feet, stuck out from an armchair in front of the television; and snotty Jason, tottering towards her.

'Who is it? All right, I'm coming.'

Patsy knew her mum could never think it was anyone she'd be pleased to see. They were down to the bare bone of contacts with the outside. Tired, depressed, and bad-tempered, even in the sunshine, there wasn't a knock in the world which could bring a pleasant surprise, no smiling relation or win on the pools.

As Patsy squinted through, her mother's legs appeared, dark veins growing out of blue slippers.

'It ain't you, Patsy, is it? What you doing here at this time?'

Patsy stood up from the letter-box. She shivered on the concrete landing. What was the use? She should've known better than to even try. They'd never let her go. She'd still end up sitting at the front of someone else's class on the day.

'Well, come in then, girl. You ill, or something?'

'No. It's the outing.'

'What outing? It ain't today, is it?'

'No. . . .' Patsy squeezed in through the narrowly opened door and let Jason have a couple of swinging bashes at her. It didn't do to upset Jason.

'What's up, then?' Mrs Green frowned and put a hand across her forehead. 'You are a problem, Patsy.'

'It's the *outing*,' Patsy repeated, her eyes trying to force out a meaning which was private from Eddie Green in the other room. 'I'm s'posed to take the paper today or I can't go.'

Jason thumped her again and then sat with a bump on the floor.

'Oh, was it today? I can't keep track of everything. . . .' Blind to Patsy's special look Mrs Green shuffled back into the kitchen on the right. 'Can't you see I've got baby's dinner to do?' She left Patsy stranded on an island of flattened rug, looking through the door at Eddie Green's legs.

No. Her mum wasn't going to help. Well, that wasn't new. She hadn't really thought she would. Eddie Green and that baby had turned her into someone else altogether from the person she'd been in the old days, when they'd just been on their own. Patsy tasted that familiar bitterness in her mouth. How could one little slug like Eddie Green make all the difference?

All right, then! Patsy suddenly felt defiant. Let him be as horrible as he liked: she was going to have a bloody good try. Why should she miss out on everything? She walked to the living-room and stood in the doorway. He'd heard her all right. Now let him take some notice.

There he was, sitting in his armchair with his paper, like an up-patient in the hospital, white-faced, small, and staring at her already. Deliberately, he folded the paper and tucked it between a bare arm and his white singlet, as if he were about to get up and go. But he didn't move anywhere. He hardly ever did. He just sat, as always: the lazy beast who even made you go and stand by him for a smack.

'What's all this about?' he asked.

He'd read all his paper and he was going to settle to this, Patsy knew. He loved the power he had in the flat. He might have been the laughing stock of the amusements down in 'Dreamland', like some of the Margate kids had said, but he'd wormed his way into being the boss in Patsy's house.

She stayed where she was in the doorway, her resolve beginning to go again as she leaned against the woodwork.

''Ave they sent you 'ome?' he asked. 'Bloody cheek!'

Patsy nodded. 'Mr Lamb says sorry, but he's got to know today, or else I can't go.'

'Oh, does 'e? Interfering again. And does 'e know the circumstances? I don't suppose 'e knows 'ow you 'ave to be kept in line. 'E doesn't 'ave the washing to do like your mother does. . . .'

13

Patsy said nothing. She'd had two good nights, but she wouldn't remind him yet, not till he'd had all his say. Her only chance was to give him the pleasure of keeping her dangling.

'Perhaps 'e doesn't know 'ow 'ard life is, with me under the doctor, and your mother's 'eadaches, and the boy to see to—without 'aving all the extra work you make.'

Patsy hung her head a little, thinking of the time when her mum might have come in from the kitchen to remind him how she hadn't done it for two nights. She would have taken her side once, when he'd first come, before she'd had the new baby. But there was no real chance of that now. All Patsy could hear was Jason banging a cupboard door open and shut, open and shut, and she knew she was on her own with him.

'I don't understand it, you going back to them baby ways. And I told you, didn't I? I ain't gonna 'ave it.' He pulled his paper out from under his arm as if that were it, as if he'd said no, finally. 'Any'ow, no one can say I ain't a fair man. Was you dry last night?'

'Yeah,' she said quietly. And the night before, and all, she thought. But he knew that. He kept a note of it somewhere.

'All right, give us your paper and I'll think about signing it.'

Strewth, what had come over him, then? He'd given in, for some reason. She'd expected a good shout with the strings of his neck all standing out, and then a 'no' at the end of it.

Unless not having the paper was part of his trick.

'I 'aven't got it. It was on the bottom of that letter....'

'Well, I 'aven't got it, 'ave I? I expect you to know where these things are. Still, if you can't be bothered to find it, I can't sign it, can I?' He flapped his paper open and assumed an interest in a page of second-hand cars.

Patsy whirled into the kitchen and rummaged through a drawer above Jason's head.

'Mind that baby....'

'It's the letter....' But at that moment her mum was busy with a pan of carroty mush, and Patsy had to search on her own. No, there was no duplicated note from the school; but chance suddenly turned up the writing pad of blue Basildon Bond. Patsy grabbed it and rummaged some more for a ball-point before running back to Eddie Green.

'It's been thrown out,' she said; 'but a note'll do.' She held out the pad, which Eddie Green stared at without moving, as if he were being served with a court order. Patsy folded back the cover and clicked the ball-point for him.

'Oh, yeah?' he said. 'So I've gotta write the 'ole thing now, 'ave I?' He put his paper down. 'Come round this side.'

Patsy stood where he told her. Then as if from nowhere his hand shot out, the paper on his lap crumpled, and a hard, stinging, slap caught Patsy's upper arm, rocking her off balance.

Christ! Ow! A stream of abuse sprang to Patsy's lips. But somehow, she said nothing. As her heart thumped and her arm stung hot she kept her mouth in a tight line—because now she knew there was a good chance that he'd write it. The next smack, on top of the first, would hurt ten times as much, and she braced herself for that, but if he was doing this, he was going to let her go. That was the way his mind worked.

'And that's what you'll get, and more of it, if you let your mum and me down again. You got this one chance, and damn me if I ain't a fool to be this soft with you....'

Patsy nodded behind a blur of tears.

'No more o' them wet beds!' he said.

She shook her head.

'Right. Now, what am I supposed to write on this?' He took the pen and the pad from her and circled a series of pre-writing movements above it.

Patsy looked at him. The spiteful swine. Who did he think he was? He wasn't her dad; nobody was. He was just some horrible bloke who'd conned her mum down in 'Dreamland' one night, and turned everything upside down—upside down his way.

And one day, for all this, when she was grown up and didn't wet the bed any more, she'd get him.

Yes, she'd get him one day. That was a promise. Or she'd get away first: make her secret dream come true.

How far had he got? His writing was slower than hers. Patsy looked at the paper, where his white and brown fingers were sloping the neat address. He hadn't even got to 'Dear Sir' yet. He was going to have to be told what to say; slowly. It was going to take ages. But who cared about that? She could run back along the creek path at top speed, and still get there in time for her dinner: straight past the shining boat, and the barmy, and not stop for a second on the way.

He was looking up at her. 'Well?' he was demanding.

At that moment, almost like fainting, her head light and her legs weak, Patsy put two random thoughts together in her brain: and they created something which made her throat go tight at the very thought of it. At the risk. But without daring to think out the consequences, slowly, in a barely controlled voice, she started to tell him what to put in the letter.

2

Kenny Granger, rough dried, sat on the stone staircase between the fourth and fifth floors. It was a good place to be, private, warm even, today; quiet and comfortable, and well away from the busy up and down of the lifts. His river swim had made him feel better. It was just the sock that worried him now; the sock lost because of his stupid rush to get undressed and in the water before anyone stopped him; and it was keeping him there, thinking up a good excuse, before he banged through the stairs door and walked home along the landing. But his bellyache had gone a long while back; it had gone that morning as soon as the streets had been empty of other kids; and since then—apart from the sock—today had been a good day, he thought. It had been too warm for him to feel all that hungry, and the river had carried his size as if it didn't exist. He hadn't heard one shout of 'Fatso' all day, and that was worth a rotten sock, he reckoned.

He stood up and wriggled his checks further down over his tight thighs, to let the legs cover his ankles a bit. Anyway, he couldn't do more, and it should just about do to get him into his bedroom for a quick change. Not that he was all that worried. He just didn't want her crying all over him again. He rubbed his hands on the dusty wall to grime himself up a bit, and then he barged through the door. He took his shuffling short steps along the landing—the walk his father hated, the comfortable movement which kept his thighs from rubbing and chafing too much—and he stopped at his door only long enough to fish the key on its damp string from around his neck.

Kenny's mind was filled with the thought of his own

17

deception and a certain something that he'd seen, so he hardly heard the lift doors shutter behind him, or Mr Lamb from the school get out a floor too soon and start looking along the landing for Patsy Bligh's number.

A short staircase later and Mr Lamb was finally ringing at the tight wound-up bell of number twenty-four. He took sideways glances along the landing in each direction before he faced the door, rocking forward on to his toes. Nothing. he rang again, and took a piece of paper out of his pocket ready to write a note.

'Yes?' The door was suddenly open a crack and a narrow strip of woman was there, keeping a toddler back with her legs.

'Mrs Green?'

'Yes.'

'It's Patsy. I'm Mr Lamb from the school. Her teacher. Is Patsy home, Mrs Green? I'm just checking.'

'No, she's not here. But she won't be long. Why?' Her narrowed eyes narrowed down further. 'Has she been playing up?' Her voice was hot and tired, but there was an aggressive edge.

'Oh, no, nothing like that. She's always as good as gold.' He leant on the doorpost, looking as if he weren't worried. 'No . . . but did she come home at dinner time, with a message about the trip?'

'Yes, that's right. And Mr Green signed it, and sent her straight back with it. He said she could go all right. . . .'

'Really? Oh . . .' Mr Lamb swallowed. 'But she hasn't come back to school, Mrs Green. We haven't seen her all afternoon.'

Mrs Green's head was shaking and the door was open wide. 'Eh? That's not right. You'll have to come in,' she said. 'You'll have to tell Mr Green. . . .'

'Of course: but don't worry: she's probably gone off with a friend, that's all. Enjoying the sun . . .' With a relaxed look on his face, and his hands clenched tight inside his jacket pockets, Mr Lamb went in through the door.

Eddie Green was sitting frowning in his armchair, dominating the room, his arms stretched out along the chair's arms like a king.

'Who's he?' he asked his wife, taking no notice of the frown on her face.

'I'm Mr Lamb, from the school. I've just called to check on. . . .'

'It's Patsy,' Mrs Green said. 'She's gone missing, Eddie!'

Jason opened his mouth in a yell, clutching at his mother's leg.

'Don't be alarmed. It's never as bad as it sounds,' the teacher reasoned. 'It rarely is. She's probably just out playing with someone. . . .'

'She 'asn't been seen since she left here.' Mrs Green's voice was raised slightly, and she was bending towards her husband.

But the small man seemed to be still savouring the situation. 'Gone missing?' he demanded. 'What the 'ell does she mean by "gone missing"?' He stared hard at Mr Lamb, cutting Patsy's mother out of the conversation.

Mr Lamb was as brief—and as calm—as he could manage. 'Well, apparently, after Patsy left here with your permission slip she decided to stay out of school. She must have thought she'd go off and play in the sun instead of coming back. But really all we need to do is find out who her friends are and see who she's with. . . .' He got out a pen and turned back to Mrs Green, ready to take down a few names and addresses. He raised his eyebrows.

But Eddie Green wasn't prepared to move so quickly. 'Just 'old on a minute,' he said. 'Not so fast. Are you telling me that after I'd gone to all that trouble to write a special note to say she could go on your outing, she never brought it back to you? She never came back with it at all?'

Mr Lamb shifted his weight. 'Yes, but who knows what

goes on in children's minds? I wouldn't put too much significance on the note. . . .'

'You leave me to put what significance where I like,' Eddie Green snapped. He pointed at the teacher. 'Listen, you sent 'er 'ome to pester me for a note, and then when she got what she was after she just cleared off. . . .'

'Eddie, she might be hurt somewhere!' Patsy's mother urged. 'She wouldn't just go off. . . .'

'Oh, wouldn't she? Selfish little cow, that one. All the bloody work she makes!' He looked at them both, hard, and with an air of finality he slid his newspaper out from the side of his chair. 'Well, she can stay out for all I care. And if she don't want to come back, that's all right with me!' He started reading again, fiercely.

'Oh, Eddie!' Mrs Green cried. 'Help us find her. . . .'

But Eddie Green wasn't going to bother even to say no.

An air of aggressive awkwardness filled the room. Mr Lamb tried to be positive.

'Friends of hers,' he said to Mrs Green. 'Who might she have seen at dinner time to go off with? Anyone off sick in the flats? Any aunts or uncles or grandparents in the district?'

'No,' Mrs Green began sniffing. 'No. . . .' She was trembling slightly now. 'Only Kenny . . . underneath . . . he's more out of school than in. No, we haven't got no relations. Oh, my God. . . .' The woman suddenly dipped, as if her legs had gone; but she pulled herself up.

'Come on, Mrs Green. It's early yet. She's all right, a million to one. But we'll just make sure.' He moved towards the door, supporting her by the elbow.

Jason started crying again, a dry screech, and he aimed a wild fist at the teacher's leg.

'Stop that, you!' Mrs Green suddenly shouted; and she pulled Jason back with a surprising jerk. 'Behave yourself! We've got to find our Patsy. . . .'

She turned her back on Eddie Green and went on to the landing to work out the number of Kenny's flat below: while

Jason sat on the floor, and grizzled, and looked at his father; and mild surprise was in both their eyes.

Kenny was in his bedroom. After being stopped by his anxious mother—already made-up, he noticed, for his father coming in, her face shaded to take the plumpness off—and after the usual questions about what he'd done at school, what he'd had for his dinner, he'd finally got to be on his own. And he was still searching untidily for another sock when the door chimes rang. He didn't realize he'd heard them until later, and he'd got as far as sitting on his bed, awkwardly pulling on a sock, when his bedroom door suddenly opened and his mother was there. She was blinking a lot, and there was a softly pleading strain in her voice.

'Kenny, love, will you come in here, please? I want you a minute.' She was sounding all the ends of the words.

Oh, blast! Someone was here. He'd been seen. Or told on. If people weren't laughing at him there was nothing some of them liked better than making his father row with his mother for her giving in to him, for not seeing he got to school.

He heaved himself up and looked at her. Yeah. She'd seen the sock. Something was clicking in her head, because already she'd got that hurt look on her face. She held the bedroom door open for him.

As he passed by her, and he saw for himself who was there, she told him. 'This teacher's come from your school, Kenny. He wants to know if you've seen Patsy from upstairs this afternoon. Did you see her coming home from school or anything?'

Kenny's eyes opened wide. 'Patsy? No,' he lied. ' 'Aven't seen her for days.' Well, how could he say exactly when he *had* seen her, just before his swim, her picking flowers when he was hiding behind a fence with no clothes on? And then later. . . . He stared hostility at Mr Lamb.

Mr Lamb smiled at him. The two of them met in public

places like the dining hall and the playground; but they were no more than figures to each other; the teacher, and the boy from a different class.

'Have you seen Patsy at all today, Kenny?' Mr Lamb asked. 'She was in the playground this morning, wasn't she?'

'I never saw her.' Kenny looked at his mother. 'There's thousands of kids in there.'

'You were at school today, were you?' Mr Lamb, already jingling the coins in his pocket, sounding ready to go, had suddenly frowned and was looking significantly at Mrs Granger.

'Yeah!' Kenny breathed in wheezily, and the skin round his mouth began to tingle.

'Because you said "*in* the playground: thousands of kids *in* there". Most children in school talk about going *out* there, *out* to play.' Mr Lamb smiled, like a lawyer in a courtroom film. 'It depends where you're standing, doesn't it? Inside or outside....'

'Yeah. I was there.' Kenny nodded, and tried to frown innocently: but, as usual, that was hard to do: his broad face never helped him to be a convincing liar, somehow. Anyway, it wasn't much use pretending. The teacher would check on him now: and his mum had looked as if she knew again, from the start.

'Kenny!' she said. 'Tell the teacher the truth. Was you at school today or wasn't you?'

Kenny stared at the floor.

'You wasn't, was you?'

Slowly, he shook his head.

Mr Lamb spoke quietly. 'Well, where were you? Who did you see?' Kenny began to feel reassured that he wasn't the main concern. Well, he wouldn't be, would he, after what he'd seen....

'I was around. Just mucking about. I felt a bit sick....'

'So where were you mucking about?' Still quiet and gentle.

'Along the walk, by the river....'

'And did you see Patsy Bligh? Around dinner time, or this afternoon?'

'Yeah, I saw her,' Kenny said finally, still to the floor. 'She was picking some flowers: and talking to this bloke. . . .' It was true, wasn't it? Better to tell them a harmless part of the truth, then you didn't get tripped up.

'Oh!' Mrs Granger's hand had flown to her mouth in a dramatic gesture, and her green eyes stared horror at Mr Lamb. 'Kenny, love, you tell the teacher everything you saw—or you know I'll have to tell Daddy all about this.' Her hand went back to her mouth.

Kenny nodded, and he swallowed, and he grabbed what seconds he could for thinking out exactly how much he should tell them about Patsy Bligh.

An hour later, in the office of Maurice Greenslade's scrap-yard, there were two conversations going on at once: the one the police constable was trying to have with the simple man, and the crackling communication between two staccato voices on his lapel radio, which had the man's attention. Finally, although P.C. White wanted to keep in touch, he switched the radio off.

'Oh,' said the man, 'where they gone? I want people back.' He made a move towards the press-button on the walkie-talkie, but the policeman shifted his position slightly.

'Well, you talk to me, Eric, then you can hear some more, all right?'

Eric rubbed his hand. His face went sulky and he looked across at Mr Greenslade for some support. But there was none. Mr Greenslade was looking at Eric with new, hard eyes.

'All right, you say you can't remember who you saw.'

Eric nodded, and smiled, as if he were pleased to be understood at last.

'But can you remember where you got this flower?' P.C. White drew the cornflower up out of Eric's buttonhole and held it delicately between his fingertips, like a scientific specimen.

'Pretty flower.'

'Yes, I know it's pretty, Eric. You like pretty things, do you?'

Eric nodded.

'So what about the pretty girl? Did you see her, Eric?'

Eric frowned. 'Pretty flower,' he said. 'Pretty girl.' He was suddenly smiling, and nodding.

'Yeah,' said the policeman. 'Both pretty.'

Holding the flower in his right hand he operated the walkie-talkie with his left.

Eric's eyes looked expectant, for the treat.

'203 to control,' P.C. White muttered into it. 'Forget sending the W.P.C. I'm bringing him down now. Show him the clothing. He's got a bit to tell us, this one, and the sooner we hear it the better, I reckon.'

The voice crackled something back; and Eric laughed aloud, enjoying it and waiting for some more. But there was none.

'Come on, Eric,' said the policeman. And the man was led gently away, his head still bent in the hope of hearing a voice.

3

As the spent sun hung over the oil refinery, deep red and finally permitting itself to be stared at, Patsy lay on the deck with her head on her arms and thought of all the times she'd seen that same sun through her bedroom window in the flat. She'd stared out at it from the prison of her room—more often than she'd wanted, locked up in there for some crime or other—and now, in this sudden freedom, she felt an odd elation. Floating here at Queenborough, with everyone going out of their way to be nice to her, it was almost as if there was too much kindness for her to cope with.

It was quiet and peaceful now. Some of the group had gone ashore to the pub and the others were below, talking quietly. Only Joe, who owned the *Dame Sybil*, was on the deck with Patsy, and he was sitting cross-legged in the bows, rubbing down a blister in the varnish.

Patsy looked at the sun wriggling red in the water, and she thought of that time earlier in the day when the glare had been too much to take, when everyone had been squinting and frowning, and she'd thought they'd say no. But now the remembering was delicious, because even disappointments could be savoured when they turned out all right in the end; and especially to be relished tonight was the thought of telling it all in triumph to Mrs Broadley's kind smile, when Patsy got to Margate on Wednesday. What would it sound like to someone else? It was hard to tell—because it all seemed like a dream already, the way the crazy plan had worked. . . .

As Patsy had been running back along the path from the flats she'd refused to let her brain work out the if's and but's. She'd know for sure when she turned the last corner, she'd

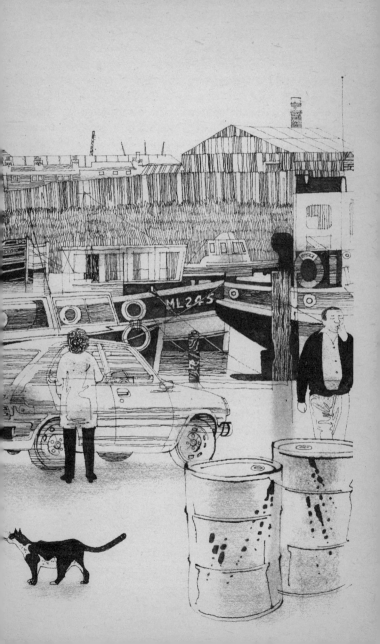

told herself. Until then there was just a faint hope, trembling inside like the heart of a chick, too weak to take the strain of thinking about things too much. Not far now, she'd thought as she ran. Then either the boat would be there, or that small creek would be the emptiest stretch of water she had ever seen in her life.

Hardly daring to look, and at the last second pretending she didn't care anyway, Patsy ran round the corner. She even put on speed, ready to carry on running if it weren't there. She'd go straight past, she decided, and do her crying later. But it was. It was there. She wanted to shout. The shining boat lay rocking gently on the water like some royal barge which wouldn't sail without the queen. She dropped the Co-op bag she was carrying. 'Good!' she said aloud. 'Thank....' But her words stuck there. Yes, the boat might still be in the creek, but now the small deck was crowded with extra people, and the one person she wanted to see, she couldn't. Oh, no! She was probably still inside, Patsy thought: she was probably underneath trying to take hold of that big box of grocery stuff those two men were wriggling through the doorway. Oh, blast! Well, that was that, wasn't it? It wouldn't be any use showing up now, because that girl Jenny was her special link with the boat, and starting again from scratch with these others would be impossible. It was like going to some girl's party and finding a load of strangers there, who all knew the girl better than you did, and just sat there looking at you funny when you spoke to them. In the end even the girl turned against you.

She eyed them up carefully, frowning like a fisherman looking for shapes beneath the surface, considering the remote chance of something coming out of this now.

There were four people altogether, all loud and relaxed as they called and laughed. Everything was noise and movement, but Patsy was noticing things—the brown shoulders of the girl, and her long hair, thick and black; and the two men at the wheel-house, all jeans, bottoms and bare backs as they bent awkwardly over the heavy box, laughing, calling for help—and getting none—from a skinny young man on the bank with his plimsolls in the water. This one, a bit sharp-featured, but with tight blond hair like the nap on a tennis ball, kicking away at the Thames as if it were a paddling pool—Patsy liked the look of him. But she didn't give much for her chances any more. She couldn't make a move, or even think of a move to make. It was all very different, this second time.

She knew that noisy banter: she heard it when people came back to the flats from the pub—and she knew so well how it wrapped them round like a layer of cotton wool. There wasn't much chance of getting through to them. Her own vague picture of Jenny and herself floating down river to Margate on the shining deck had been no more than the wildest dream, she could see that now. She shivered, even in the heat. Her elation at the boat still being there had gone, and her hopes were too thin now to cast the faintest shadow. Her little bit of cunning with Eddie Green had all been for nothing.

But for a moment longer her feet stayed where they were; and as she considered herself for a moment before moving off, she became aware that she was standing there still clutching at the hot sting which mottled her arm. God, that had hurt! That pig, Eddie Green! So after all that it was back to him, then, was it? Back to crawling about like a whipped puppy over a wet bed? Was that all there was left for her again? She drew her shoulders up and let them drop in a huge gesture of despair. It would have been better never to have seen the boat than to have to look at all this happy activity which had nothing to do with her.

Patsy suddenly tightened her mouth. All right, so who cared how silly she looked? What the hell had she got to lose? It was worth one wild chance, wasn't it?

It was like the first jump off a high board. Sudden. No going back.

'Wotcha!' she called to the man who was dangling his feet. 'That water wet, is it?'

The foot-dangler smiled and lifted his heavy plimsolls, bending his knees up like a toddler to see the water running out of the ventilation holes. When there was no more to come he squinted up at the girl above him.

'Back where it came from,' he said with a giggle.

'Yeah. Here, will you tell Jenny I've got that letter she wanted?'

'Eh? Who, our Jenny?'

The others had got the groceries through the wheel-house now and their ears had pricked up at the sound of a familiar name. One of the men looked across at her, taking up the conversation from the foot-dangler. He seemed the sort who'd be in charge. But he was smiling, and more than affable.

'Hello, sweetheart,' he said. 'Are you a friend of *our* Jenny?'

'Yeah. Sort of.' He seemed nice, Patsy thought; a good-looking bloke, dark-haired and tall, with only a bit of a frown line between his eyes; looked like a proper actor, on the telly.

He moved lightly across the deck and came over to lean his hand against the wooden shoring. He stumbled just once, and a suppressed burp watered his eyes before he could look up at her properly.

'Well, what a small world,' he laughed.

Patsy looked quickly at them all. The foot-dangler was sitting and looking; the golden girl was leaning and looking; and the other man at the hatch—an older man with an outdoor face—was squatting on a box and looking. They were all looking at her.

'Want some good news?' she asked brightly. 'I've got the letter for Jenny. My mum and dad definitely said I could come....' She smiled widely and lit up her eyes.

'Really?' said the actor. He looked round at the others. 'Did you hear that?' The foot-dangler laughed, and the girl smiled and shrugged her shoulders.

'Yeah, here it is,' Patsy hurried on. She reached into her Co-op bag and brought out the Basildon Bond. 'And I've brought my things....' She was determined to force this

30

through with speed and energy now, or be back in school in time for second dinners. 'Only Jenny said I had to have it.' She handed the sheet of notepaper down.

The golden girl came over and draped a long arm round the actor's neck to read it with him; while the older man at the wheel-house called softly down the steps.

'It's about that kid,' Patsy hurried on, this sudden new instinct for getting what she wanted telling her she mustn't let the pressure go now. 'Tracey in your play. My dad says it's all right with him for me to come and be in it. See, we're on 'oliday next week, and Jason's just gone in the 'ospital, and they're gonna be up and down all week, and my dad says yes. It'll help out, he reckons. He's giving his permission, there. . . .' She pointed to the note, which the actor was trying to get into focus. There was a moment's silence—apart from the splash of plimsolls kicking in the water again, and a new whispering at the wheel-house as Jenny's hat appeared.

But Patsy wasn't going to let anything go against her in a lull. As if everything had been decided, she threw her carrier bag on to the deck and climbed down after it.

'Oh, darling,' the actor said, 'we're going miles away. We're not doing it here. Are we?' He turned to the girl with him, who made a bad luck face. 'I don't think we can just . . . take you off. . . .'

Saying nothing, and looking as if she weren't sure whether it was safe even to smile at Patsy, Jenny had come up and was reading the note, and now the older man joined her. It gave Patsy a few seconds in which to sit herself down in a small and pathetic hunch on the boat's deck. She wasn't going to leave a trick untried. It was do-or-die now.

'Lovey, you got it wrong, didn't you?' Jenny said after reading the letter. 'My fault, my fault,' she told the others. 'Big mouth. But I never dreamed . . .' She sighed. 'Oh, lordy.' She crouched down beside Patsy, shading them both with her sun hat. 'Oh, hell, what can I say?'

The other girl spoke. 'Well, it says here quite plainly, "My

31

daughter has permission to go on the tour of Kent next week". *And* it's got an address. *And* it's signed, by Eddie Green. Is that your dad?'

Patsy nodded. He was married to her mum and he hit her, so she supposed he was, in a way.

'Well, what more do you want?' the girl asked the actor. 'It's dated today. That's legal. That's permission, I would have thought. And we *could* use a Tracey, let's face it. It's a much better curtain with the kid there: so why look a gift horse in the mouth? I say take her.' She looked down at Patsy. 'You're house-trained, aren't you?'

Patsy nodded again. She had been.

'Well, what's all the fuss about?' The girl did a sudden Peter Pan leap across to the young man with his plimsolls in the water. 'What does Bob say? Eh?'

'Don't ask me, I don't make decisions.' Then, with a different, professional tone, he quietly added, 'But that is a good moment when it works.' He looked at the water again. 'So long as it doesn't present other problems.' He shrugged, and started kicking again, with more splashes than before.

Everything was suddenly very serious.

'Well. . . .' said the actor.

'Well, Peter, whatever you decide to do, do it in a hurry, old son. This tide won't wait for above another fifteen minutes, not with my draught. She'll be stuck on this mud if we don't cast off pretty lively. . . .' The older man was looking out at the water, and rubbing his chin.

Patsy stayed in her hunched position, not moving a muscle. She found it hard to breathe quietly.

'Do you live far? We ought to check,' the actor said.

'Yeah, over there.' Patsy pointed vaguely towards the flats, giving her arm plenty of elevation to indicate more distance, and holding the pose in a quite theatrical way.

'Really, there's no time, Peter,' the older man said. 'Time and tide wait for no man, and all that. It really does boil down to putting her up on the path now, or taking her with us. . . .'

'Are you on the 'phone?'

Patsy shook her head, deliberately, as if that were the way to be, not on the 'phone.

The actor passed the back of his hand across his brow. He was clearly regretting that final drink.

'And you all think this is legal enough?' He waved the letter at the others.

'Yes!' they all chorused—all but the man who was busy making preparations to cast off.

'Well, I suppose we can write and give details of where we are, and when we'll be back. . . . .'

'Yes. Yes, we can easily do that,' Jenny said, getting up. She smiled at Patsy. There was a long, indefinite, silence. 'Well, come on, then.' A flurry of movement. 'Happy ending!' she said.

Patsy nodded. She hoped so. God, how she hoped so.

'Better put that letter in a safe place,' the older man called. 'And stand by to cast off! For crying out loud, you're all worse than useless when you've had a drink.'

The actor stuffed the letter in his jeans pocket. 'You will be . . . all right . . . won't you?'

Patsy nodded, demurely, like all the little heroines she'd seen on the television. But inside she felt as if she might burst: and she had to fight against an enormous desire to shout out to Eddie Green the loudest message ever heard on that stretch of water.

People started moving about, and there was a soggy splash as two plimsolled feet landed on the deck.

'Yes, ladies and gentlemen,' Bob wiped his hands forward on his nap of hair, 'I think there's a chance this young lady's quite a clever little actress.' And he went below to lie down.

Now Patsy's arm was red again, not with the smack any longer but with sucking on it as she rested on the deck, remembering. She tried to rub it away. Perhaps a dream coming true always paralysed you like that, where you felt nothing with your body, not the sucking, not the chill of the evening. Or perhaps she was just tired. But was she really here in this little cut off Queenborough—more than half-way back to Margate? Or would she wake in a minute to that terrible feeling of guilt, and the cold sweat of panic about the wet bedclothes?

She shivered as the evening air came cool off the water. No, it was all true. She was where she was, because she could remember the details: the watery pop of the exhaust, like a drowning motor-bike, the flatness of the water, as low and wide as you could have it, the rusty dribbling giant of the grey ship which had dwarfed them as it went gliding by; then the casual talk of the Medway—Eddie Green's old backyard— which had chilled her for a moment; and finally, the fish fingers and Smash which Jenny had cooked in relays for their tea, with the warm white wine which tasted of coconuts. No, you couldn't go back into memory like that in your dreams. She was Patsy Bligh. She was on the *Dame Sybil* down in Queenborough. And she had run off from home, with her tracks as neatly covered as anyone could wish. There was no way she would turn over in a minute and hear Eddie Green's whining morning cough. No way. That was something she was never going to hear again—not for as long as she lived.

4

It would have been dead easy for Kenny to cover the mirror on the front of his wardrobe—there were plenty of posters about and Sellotape was handy enough—but as much as his reflection brought him down, his pride wouldn't let him hide it. That would have been like doing away with himself, and he was a long way off hating himself enough for that. Besides, he had another answer.

He looked at his reflection, hard. He'd always been the fat one. There had never been a time when he hadn't puffed last behind the others, or given up half-way; and people had made jokes about him since before he knew what jokes were. He was the pig, the elephant, the hippopotamus, the balloon, the ton weight, the human dustbin, Tubby, Porky, Fatso; he was everything that was big or heavy or greedy; and he was expected to laugh at all of it, to take it all in good part and never get upset by their great humour. He was a fat cry-baby or a bad sport if he did. 'Can't you take a joke?' they'd sneer—'Fatso?' So Kenny didn't get upset any more: he took it when he had to with a slow smile he'd practised to make them think he was thick as well as fat. But his best trick of all was just not to be there; to be on his own with his own thin thoughts, where no one could remind him all the time of how impossible it was for him to be like the rest. And those thoughts of his were mostly about one day when he'd finally show them: one day when he wouldn't have to take it any more: one day when he'd stare some joker coldly in the eye, and with immense strength reach out his hands and. . . .

He sat on his bed and stared at himself. So, it looked like Patsy upstairs was off on that plan of hers, now. Lucky her.

35

But his turn would come. One day his plan would work out, too, he told himself. One day it would.

There was a knock on his door. Oh, no. . . .

'Kenny. . . .'

'Yeah?'

'Oh, Kenny, love. . . .'

Oh God, no. Her voice spilled out disappointment as if she was filled up to there with it. 'What?'

'You know what, Kenny,' she said, coming in. 'Why didn't you go to school, today?'

He looked at her and blinked; like a shrug but less energetic.

'You've been down the baths all day, haven't you, Kenny? That's where you left your sock. . . .'

He blinked again. Well, she'd better believe that. It was a darned sight better than being in the river: she'd fuss and worry something terrible over that.

'Why, then, Kenny? Why? Do you want Mummy to have to go up to court? And what about Daddy? Think if *he* had to go to court because you're missing your schooling.' Her voice caught on the words and her eyes sparkled beneath the broad green crescents of colour-shadow. She dabbed at them carefully with a little lacy handkerchief. 'You know I don't like worrying Daddy about you. He works so hard for us, all those long hours so we can have our colour telly and our little treats while he's out. He doesn't want his supper spoilt every night by having to get upset about you, does he?' Kenny stayed looking at his hands, laced at the finger tips and held down on his lap. 'Now that schoolteacher's bound to tell Mrs Daulton—and I'll have to go up the school again. Kenny, love, what can I tell them?' She was sitting down and pleading now, squeezed into the wicker chair under the window. 'Why don't you want to go to school? Can't you do your lessons? Do you want to be put away—taken away from Mummy and Daddy?' The tears had welled up again. 'Is anyone hitting you? Is that it?'

36

'No. . . .' He looked away from her, not believing that she didn't know. *She* was fat, that's why *he* was fat. Hadn't she had all the aggravation, too?

'Well, I don't know, Kenny. You're a big worry to Mummy.' She worked her way out of the chair and stood up.

Kenny watched her in disgust. Thank God, he thought, she's going now. . . . But she suddenly sat down again, next to him on the bed, and grabbed his hands in her own.

'Now listen, Kenny: if I don't tell Daddy this time, will you promise me—on your word of honour—not to miss no more school? Will you make me that promise, Kenny?' She looked hard at him. *Please*, her eyes were pleading, *please*.

Kenny took a quick look at her. That was easy. He'd say anything to stop her crying, sitting and rocking and fussing over him the way she did sometimes, all upset and acting as if she was the kid and he was the grown-up. But making some sort of a promise didn't mean he had to keep it. He'd decided that a long time back. When you were on your own like he was you made your own rules.

'Yeah. All right.'

She squeezed his hands. 'Promise?'

'Yeah.'

'Good boy, Kenny. Good. That's definitely the last time, eh?'

'Yeah.'

'Good boy.'

Kenny tried to look away. As long as she didn't cuddle and kiss him, that was all. And he hated her staring at him like that, all sincere and pleading—and then all relieved because she didn't have to upset Daddy. It gave him the shivers. Come on, clear off now! He'd said what she wanted. Go and touch up your eyes before Daddy comes in!

But she didn't move. Still she sat there, close and pressing. He had to pull his hands out of hers—and still she stayed.

'Little Patsy,' she said. 'What was exactly going on when

37

you saw her, Kenny? It all sounds a bit funny. That poor mother must be worried to death upstairs.'

Kenny tried to keep any expression off his face while he racked his brain. He had to think what he'd said to Mr Lamb. He had to be careful. He mustn't let too much out, if he could manage it, because he was sworn to secrecy about Patsy's dream. He mustn't say what he'd really seen.

'I dunno,' he said. 'It was one of them loonies. He was just talking to her. She picked some flowers, then she talked to this bloke. Then I cleared off....' He had to keep it vague; she mustn't know he'd dived into the river just then or they'd be back to all the fussing again. And above all else he mustn't breathe a word of what he'd seen later.

She sat looking at him, probably thinking her own thoughts about what could have happened. But inside he was screwing up. Every second it got worse. How could he get rid of her? It was so close and shut in, the two of them in this little room, her sitting right next to him on the bed and dipping him in towards her. He wanted space, freedom, being on his own with no one touching him. This just made him hot and gasping for breath; it made him want to push out, and shout.

He'd just have to give her something else, to go away and chew over: something to get himself out of this. Quick!

Perhaps just a bit of the truth wouldn't hurt. 'Well, I think there was a boat there, in the creek. Yeah, there definitely was.' He stood up himself, away from her sweet-smelling warmth. 'Tell you what, I'll go and see if it's still there....' Straight away he knew that that was more than he should have said. Although it wasn't anything *definite* about Patsy, was it? And he had to have something to get him up and out of here for a bit.

'A boat, Kenny? Are you sure, love? There aren't many boats stop there in that muddy hole. It's enough to kill anyone, that dirty place.' She shuddered at her own dark thoughts. 'I just hope that poor little girl's not under that filthy water, I really do....'

'Yeah,' said Kenny. 'Anyway, it's worth having a look, see if it's still there: see if they saw anything....'

'Well, don't you be long, Kenny, in case someone's still lurking around....'

'No.'

Kenny closed the door of the flat behind him. Stupid old woman, he thought. He had to get out, even if it was just as far as the landing. He made for the stairs, and thought of Patsy sitting there talking to him: telling him her plans, and never laughing at him or calling him names. Well, she'd done it, she'd gone, off to that special place she'd come from. And he hadn't really said enough to spoil it for her, had he? No, of course he hadn't. And good luck to her. She deserved it.

It was only a shame his own plan couldn't be worked so quick!

Patsy's laughter was verging on hysteria. It had been a long time since anyone but Mary McArthy had tried to make her laugh, and now, like an unblocked water-pipe, it was all coming out in a surging rush. Joe, the owner of the *Dame Sybil*, could talk fast gibberish, sounds which seemed as if they'd make sense if only you could catch the words, and now he had Patsy croaking in her throat, drained by laughter. They were all there, lying and sitting in the cabin, with the portholes open to the slap of muddy water.

It was a fair-sized boat they were on: an old working barge, Joe explained, used to carrying coal in the space where they were all lounging. To Patsy it seemed nearly as big as the Deptford flat. And it was a darned sight more fun. A small lamp hissed above their heads and Ruth, the golden girl, who'd had a good evening in the pub, kept trying to blow it out: while Joe, sitting on the matting in between, was pretending to see a fantastic future in Patsy's small palm. It sounded good so far, even though she couldn't understand a word of it. Just one long hilarious life ahead.

'Joe, you'll have her sick in a minute. You're worse than

Bob for going too far.' That was Jenny, who was nursing a cigarette and blowing the smoke out through the porthole behind her.

Bob said something very rude from beneath his headache, and after a few seconds, while Patsy wound down, Pete the actor shut his notebook and called for 'lights out'.

'We've got a hard day tomorrow. Rehearsal for Patsy first, and out on the tide.'

Joe straightened up, suddenly serious. 'Yes, that's right: it's not far round to Steeple Stones, but I want to get time to check the hall before the shops shut. Just in case there's something we need....'

She might have felt exhausted by all that laughter, but talk of a rehearsal had sat Patsy up straight. It wasn't half funny how you could sometimes forget all about what you were supposed to be doing. Like reading the temperature on the school roof....

'Do you want to go somewhere before you kip down, lovey? It's awkward getting out in the night on a strange boat....'

Oh, Lord! Patsy could never entirely forget it, but she'd hidden it at the back of her mind tonight. Now Jenny had made it important again. She'd been turning down drinks all the evening, but she'd better go. She'd better take all the precautions she could.

The others talked loudly while Patsy was in there, just as they did for everyone as they went through the final ritual before bed: and then she was left to lie on the bunk with her eyes closed during the private rustle and clump of undressing down the length of the boat. The bunk was comfortable—it had the feel of her bed at home—and it was just a few moments of enforced privacy: but while she was lying there, in spite of herself she found she was thinking about Eddie Green.

It had been a bit like tonight, the evening her mum had brought him back from 'Dreamland'. That had been a first meeting, with him trying to make her laugh. Her mum's job taking the money on a kids' roundabout three nights a week had never led to cups of tea back at Mrs Broadley's before; but that night Eddie Green must have told her some really fancy tales, because he was brought in like a long-lost relation: and before six weeks had passed they were out of Mrs Broadley's and up in Deptford, in the council flat. And within the year Jason had come, and Patsy had started to wet. That's when the smackings had begun, sending her half-way across the room sometimes, and everything had turned upside down. But what was worse, Patsy's mum seemed to have forgotten the Margate days, and the afternoon walks along the front, and the nice times with Mrs Broadley. So they'd both been trapped by Eddie Green, in different ways, and they'd both changed. Whoever would have thought it'd lead to this?

'Hey, don't frown. Don't screw your eyes up. We want you looking pretty as a picture for Tracey. . . .' It was Pete bending over her. 'Good-night, Patsy.' He hesitated, as if deciding whether to kiss her on the forehead.

' 'Night.'

He didn't.

'Good-night, all. No talking!'

But they did talk, Pete as well, and Patsy listened to their tired voices and their giggles and snuffles for a while, until her own exhausted mind drifted her off into a confused dream of Eddie Green and Mrs Broadley, both on a stage. And by the time they started whispering about having brought her on the boat she was well gone, and she didn't hear Bob moaning from his bunk in the bows.

'Well, I hope she behaves herself. I'm supposed to be on holiday from kids. . . .'

But Jenny was asleep, too, by then—and nobody else answered him.

'Nothing known,' said Detective Sergeant Harris as he came back through the door of the interview room. 'And it looks like his old lady's taken it a bit hard. The doctor's indoors, and a neighbour.' He looked past Inspector Stein at Eric and went on talking about him as if he weren't sitting there. 'She can't accept the idea of her son harming a little girl.'

Eric's elbows were on the table and he supported his head on his hands. It had never been right, his head, and now it looked like a ton weight the simple man was bearing.

'Eric!' The C.I.D. man stood across the table from him, his feet apart. 'Time you was home with your mum, don't you reckon? Now, all we want to know is about that girl you were talking to: then if we're happy about it, we can take you home in a big police car—can't we, Mr. Stein?'

'I don't see why not,' the Inspector replied; 'yes, I should think so.' He slipped a slim silver cigarette case out of his uniform jacket and took out two cigarettes, holding one up behind him for Harris. 'If we can clear up this flower business to our satisfaction, and the cardigan we found, I should think we could definitely let you go home.'

Eric said nothing. He was frowning, with a sulky push to his mouth. Sergeant Harris drew up a chair and sat down.

'Look, Eric; let's all try and get this straight, eh? This girl was picking flowers, right? She was seen picking flowers, the blue ones, and she was seen sticking some in her cardigan. And then she was seen talking to a man. Now, since you had a blue flower stuck in your jacket, we presume that man was you. That was you, right?' He stabbed a finger at him, but didn't touch. 'Now you can follow that, can't you? So all you've got to do is just answer yes or no, or nod your head, and save us all the trouble of an identity parade. . . .' He leant across the table and tilted Eric's head gently under the chin so that their eyes met. His voice was low and cajoling. 'Yes or no, see. Now, Eric, did you get that flower off a young girl?'

Eric looked back at him, frowning harder, as if all this had happened too long ago to remember.

'You remember the flower, don't you?' He pushed it towards him in its plastic exhibit bag. 'Now, just yes or no, Eric. Did you take it off the young girl?'

There was a moment of stillness in the room, and a burst of laughter from somewhere a few doors away; before Eric suddenly started to shake his head vigorously, frowning his frustration.

Sergeant Harris smiled tightly. 'Oh, you didn't take it. . . .' His eyes brightened. 'Well, it's a pretty flower, isn't it? Very pretty. So did she *give* it to you? Is that what you're saying? You didn't *take* it, but she *gave* it to you. Eh?'

The full-faced policeman remained staring at the man; and as he slowly stroked his blond moustache first there was the loosening of the mouth muscles, then of the muscles which held the frown, and finally there was the slow and deliberate nod as Eric seemed to respond to being understood by someone at last.

'Good, Eric. She gave it to you, then?'

Eric nodded again, less deliberately now.

'And you stuck it down your jacket, did you?'

'Pretty flower.' Eric smiled and reached across to the sergeant's tweed jacket. 'There, then there,' he explained. He brought his hand back and in a mime put the flower down through his own buttonhole.

Detective Sergeant Harris looked at Inspector Stein under cover of stubbing his cigarette out in the glass ashtray. 'I see, Eric.' He lightened his tone. 'So, the flower, now; just to get it straight; was it stuck in her cardigan then? In a hole, or something?'

Eric nodded, but his concentration was going. 'Pretty.' For something to do, it seemed, he picked up the cornflower and tried to sniff it through the plastic.

'Not long,' Sergeant Harris said. 'We're getting somewhere now, aren't we, Eric?'

Eric stared at the flower.

'So when did she take her cardigan off, old son? Can you remember that?'

But Eric was frowning again, and another pout formed like a bruising above his mouth.

43

'Look, she gave you the flower out of her cardigan. Then the cardigan came off. We know that because we've found it: we've got the cardigan. And you've seen it, haven't you? Mr Stein showed it to you before it went for tests. Well, now, all we want to know—before we let you go home—is, did she take it off? Perhaps it was too hot, eh? Or did something else happen?'

Eric was shaking his head vigorously now, and staring at the table—as if the policeman had put a plate of something he couldn't eat in front of him.

'Now you're shaking your head. Are you saying that she was still wearing it, then, when you last saw her?'

But Eric's head was shaking more furiously.

'She wasn't wearing it?'

Now a nod, then a shake, and finally Eric started whining; a forced attempt at tears in all the confusion.

'Girl go, "bye-bye," ' he dribbled out; and he waved, a big, long-armed gesture that made the room seem too small for the three men. 'Skin,' he said, rubbing his coat sleeve. ' "Bye-bye." Skin. No card'gun.'

'*No* cardigan when she waved good-bye?'

Eric shook his head again. 'No card'gun.'

'No cardigan. She had it on when she was first talking to you . . . but when she waved good-bye she had bare arms. . . .'

Eric went back to nodding again. Till he stopped, and smiled, happy to have things sorted out, it seemed.

Detective Sergeant Harris stood up. 'Oh, dear, Eric,' he said. 'All this needs looking into. You seem to be confusing us more than helping us at the moment, old son. Which means that going home doesn't look too promising for you just yet awhile.' He jingled the change in his pocket. 'Mr Stein, I think we'd better book Eric in downstairs . . . just for a while . . . till we get things a bit more sorted. . . .'

'No problem,' said the Inspector, standing up and adjusting his smartness. 'I don't really think he's our man—that's if there's one at all. But we won't take any chances.' He walked

44

swiftly out of the room to put the arrangements for a cell in hand without delay.

'Go home!' Eric raised his voice to an angry shout.

'Not yet, old son,' said the policeman quietly. 'In a little while, perhaps. . . .'

Jason had never been shot to bed so early in all his life. Sylvia Green's nagging worry wasn't his supper, or his bowels, tonight; it was the missing Patsy who took her over to the window, out to the landing, on to the parapet; and Jason's needs were decided for him and swiftly dealt with. He was dumped, overgrown, into his cot with the sides put up and left to grind his teeth and shout behind a firmly closed door.

Eddie Green sat through the slamming in and out, Jason's screeched protests, and his wife's tearful whimpering without reaction. He looked at the *Evening Standard* or *News and Views at Six*, changing focus with his eyes but otherwise unmoved and unmoving.

'D'you reckon she could be playing with a mate somewhere? Eh, Eddie?' Sylvia kneeled beside his chair and stared into his eyes for some kind of comfort.

'Dunno,' said Eddie, giving none. 'She's asked for what she gets, that one. . . .'

'Oh, Eddie. . . .'

'Don't worry me with it. I've always done my best to discipline her.'

'I know you have, Eddie, but it's getting on for seven o'clock. . . .'

Eddie's stillness said that didn't concern him either.

But it concerned Sylvia. Suddenly, she jumped up, and ran into the kitchen to scrag her hair up under a band. 'I've gotta go,' she shouted as her nervous fingers pushed. 'This minute, Eddie, while it's light, before them drunks and down-and-outs are all over the pavements.' She worried herself into a mac, out of habit. 'Jason's with you, all right?'

Eddie Green grunted, and shifted a little in his seat.

Sylvia took the stairs rather than wait for the lift and half-walked, half-ran, around the streets. In the heat there were so many people out of doors—on balconies, in porchways, outside pubs—and there were so many children with them, that it seemed as if they'd all come out to be counted by her, sort of turning out their pockets of fivers to show they hadn't got her lost property. Running single-minded, as only a searching parent can, Sylvia got to the river walk. There was no activity there, no one looking for footprints in the mud: but then there were no men in rubber suits, either. She looked out across the grey river. 'Patsy,' she said in her throat, 'where the hell are you, Patsy?' She ran back along the path, calling 'Patsy' between the gaps in the fence, looking down into every small creek where the water inched up over the sucking mud. 'PATSY!'

Then she stopped, and she suddenly turned for home. It was abrupt; and anyone seeing her would have known it accompanied a dramatic change of mind.

Eddie Green met her with a cold stare. 'Oh, the police came,' he informed her.

'Yes?'

'Two of 'em. One and a woman.'

'Yes, yes?'

'Well, they 'aven't found 'er.' He looked back at the television for a moment. 'They wanted to know something about was she wearing a cardigan when she came 'ome for that letter, dinner time.'

'Well, what did you tell them? You told them she wasn't, didn't you?'

'No. I dunno, do I? I told them I dunno, they'd better see you about it. . . .'

For a second Sylvia Green said nothing. She stared at her husband. Then she took a step nearer to him, the fawn hair-band and raincoat suddenly in strong contrast to her reddening face. 'No, she wasn't wearing her cardigan!' she shouted. ''Course she wasn't! You 'it 'er 'ard enough on her bare arm for me and Jason to 'ear it in the kitchen, so you should know she wasn't wearing no bloody cardigan!'

Eddie Green started. ' 'Ow the 'ell do I remember? She's a bad girl. I 'ave to 'it 'er so often. And don't you start bloody shouting at....'

'And don't you give me that!' Sylvia Green's foot shot out and with her sole she rocked the armchair so that Eddie had to grip hold of the arms to prevent himself falling out. He rocked back into place facing away from the television. 'And I'll tell you this ...' Sylvia grabbed the chair in her anger and tipped it right over, a mother's superhuman strength in her, sending Eddie Green sprawling to the floor. '... I'll tell you this. While I'm ringing the police you're going out to look for my Patsy. You've sent her off, and you're going out to get her back. Or else you can start looking for someone else stupid enough to do all this for you....' She swept her arm wildly round the room. 'Do you hear me?'

It had been as sudden and as unexpected as an urban bombing. Shocked by the explosion, Eddie Green bandaged a few words together. 'All right, I was going to. I was only waiting till it was definitely serious. You know kids. She could've been playing all sorts of games up to now....'

'Well, she ain't: and nor ain't I! See here, if anything's happened to that girl I'm holding you responsible, Eddie Green! Don't you forget that!'

'All right, Sylv. All right....'

'Then you start looking—and I'll tell you, you needn't bother bloody coming back without 'er....'

Silently, Eddie Green skirted the room and went to find his belt.

'Leave the door on the latch,' Sylvia told him: and she went out of the flat again, clutching her purse in her hand.

Eddie Green returned and picked up the chair; but he didn't stop to put it back where he liked it. All at once, he had something more urgent to do.

*

47

Detective Sergeant Harris took Sylvia's call. 'Oh, yes,' he said; and, 'She wasn't? Thanks;' and, 'No, not yet, love, I'm afraid.' Then he went in to Inspector Stein. 'I think we can clear our Eric,' he told him. 'Patsy Bligh was seen at home *without* her cardigan. Whatever he says about bare arms, she was seen alive and well *after* giving him the flower. I don't think we've any call to keep him. Let him get up the hospital to see his old lady, eh?'

'O.K., Dave. No harm done. You have to be sure.... But put the river police on the alert, and send that description down the line.'

'Yes, guv....'

'And give our Eric a lift in one of the cars.'

'Right.' Sergeant Harris yawned. It was all endless, his shoulders said, as he went out through the door.

5

Being softly shaken from a deep sleep was a luxury Patsy had
forgotten: most days it was more a case of shooting up guilty
from a wet bed, all panic, worrying about him finding out:
there was no such thing as a gentle awakening to her any more.
But today was different. Coming up out of sleep, it was to
the soft sound of Jenny's voice, and it was like life a long time
ago.

'Patsy, lovey, Patsy; time to rise and shine.'

'Oh.' Yawn. 'Oh, 'ello, er....'

'Jenny.' Jenny laughed, and stroked her forehead.

'Yeah. 'Ello, Jenny....' She wriggled up, luxurious in the
warm bunk. She didn't even have to think about being dry,
because she was. That was the way it went. It was only when
you weren't that you thought about it.

'It's going to be another scorcher.'

'Great....'

'Lovely for on the boat, but God knows who'll want to
come and see a play in a stuffy hall, if this goes on....'

'Oh, they'll come,' Pete mumbled through a soft boiled
egg, over in the centre of the cabin. 'If it's only with Joe's
friends we'll be half full....'

Oh, yeah, the play. Patsy kept forgetting. Doing that part
was why they'd let her come. Not getting her back to Mrs
Broadley: that wasn't part of their plans. Well, that was no
great hardship. She was going to like doing acting. She'd be all
right; and even if she wasn't, well, it was no skin off her nose—
just as long as she didn't get taken home before they got to
Margate.

'Look, lovey, up and a quick wash, then Ruth'll do you an

egg, then chop-chop because Pete wants to do some work on your scene.'

Oh, so that was it. They were going to make sure she was O.K. before they took her any further. That was obviously what they were about; now they were all sober! Patsy didn't dawdle. She squeezed into the small washing space and pumped up a few centimetres of water to give herself a cat-lick: and while the others clumped about on deck she ate her egg and washed up her things, so that within ten minutes of being woken she was climbing out through the wheel-house to find Pete. She'd got to get this over with. She'd got to show them she could do it—and get the boat a bit nearer Margate before some busybody started nosing around.

Once outside the tension went, lifting noticeably like a short, fierce headache does when you stop eating ice-cream. The sun was shining down again as if the south of England were the Riviera, and even the muddy mouth of the Swale sparkled an intermittent blue in reflection of the clear sky. Something in Patsy responded physically to all that. And as the group's attention centred on her for twenty minutes in the mild morning warmth, and as she felt herself pleasing them, her spirits rose and wheeled on currents of good feeling, and she forgot her worries for a while.

As she saw it, Patsy's part in things wasn't big, but it was quite important. She was in at the end of the first act, and she held the centre of the stage as the curtain came across. Jenny had described it most dramatically. 'Ruth is a famous actress with a big house in the country. She's married to a big producer, but she hates him. She's wanted him out of the way for years. That's Joe. And *he* can be really nasty when he wants! Anyway, lovey, just before the end of the first act, he's found dead: a letter-opener through the heart: and guess who's suspect number one? Right! Anyway, as Ruth's about to be arrested, in comes the cleaning lady—me, of course—with my daughter—that's you. And you tell the detective—that's Bob—about a strange man you've seen in the lane.

You're all pie-eyed and innocent, and *very* convincing. And at the curtain we've got all the audience thinking again, because the man you've described is the actress's leading man. Pete, of course. And he's standing there, right under the nose of the detective, while you're saying it all. It's a load of rubbish, of course, typical comedy thriller, but played fast it gets the laughs, and it certainly has its dramatic moments. It's a real spine-chiller—and a marvellous opportunity for Bob and Pete to act their hearts out. . . .'

Patsy had read the original script. She'd been quite excited by it and hers wasn't at all a bad little part. She could definitely see how it was better for a kid to actually do it than for Jenny to have to say it for her.

She soon had the words off pat—she never had much trouble learning things—and with Bob and Ruth to talk through their lines she said her part word-perfect the first time she was asked. Just like doing an assembly at school, she thought. It was just a bit fast, Pete said—her old trouble—but that was all. The second time, though, walking it through on the slight slope of the deck, she knew she'd done it well; and the good-looking Bob was the first to pat her on the back.

'Well, that's all right, kid. That'll prickle the hairs on their necks!'

'Yes, very good, Patsy,' said Pete, genuinely pleased himself. 'Just hold that look across at me till the end. Don't move. Whatever you do, don't look away till you're certain the curtain's closed. That'll be fine.'

These drama people! Patsy thought. What a funny lot. They were all easy about bringing you miles away from home, but dead serious about where your left foot was, and the tilt of your head. Anyway, they made you feel great when you'd done it the way they wanted. And that was the only way she wanted to feel, thank you very much.

Elated with her success, she looked out and around with charitable eyes. It wasn't much of a place, this, all those big tanks of oil across the water and mud everywhere you looked;

but it was flat and open, and there was a real feeling of freedom about it, especially from the deck of the luxury boat. Compared with hanging about round the flats, keeping out of Eddie Green's way and trying to stop Jason from creating, this was like paradise, she thought. Even Kenny in his river couldn't feel as happy and as free as this.

There was more rehearsing on deck that morning, cheerfully done in the vast open-air auditorium to an audience of sea-birds; the words happily lost in the sunshine.

'All right, people, let's get under way,' Joe said eventually. 'Before the pubs open! Milk's aboard, and bread?'

Bob said they were. And the wine. . . .

'Right, then cast off from that buoy, Bob, and let's get round to Steeple Stones on the tide.'

'Have you heard of Steeple Stones?' Pete suddenly asked.

Patsy shook her head; a bit too quickly. 'Well, I've *heard* of it,' she said.

'It's nothing special, really. Lots of small boats, a harbour and a lifeboat station. But it's the tide, we have to time our comings and goings.'

Patsy looked attentive. But she could probably have told Pete about Steeple Stones. It had been a favourite bus ride from Margate when Mrs Broadley had had her. They'd been to see the lifeboat—only a little one, she remembered, not what she'd imagined—and there were nice places on the beach for sitting and eating ice-cream. And not a lot of trippers. Hardly any kids with their mums and dads on the beach: mostly locals with their boats.

'It's where old Joe comes from,' Pete was going on. 'He lived here with his wife for years, till she died. A very keen actress, Betty was, soon had him roped in to do the scenery and lights for her plays. And our Joe's been hooked on the smell of size and hot lamps ever since. Acting too. Like this week, we occasionally get him up on the stage for a few minutes.' He twisted his head to look at Joe, busy with the wheel and drawing contentedly on an old yellowing pipe.

52

Patsy looked at him, too. A bit hard to make out, Joe was. One minute—like last night—he was all over her; then another time—like today—he seemed to be deliberately keeping his distance.

Pete had stopped talking, and Patsy turned away from him and lay down on a towel. She relaxed herself like a cat, dangling an arm over the side while the sun shone down, feeling the throb of the boat through her belly. It was luxurious, and Patsy half-closed her eyes. Now there were no human voices; they had all fallen into their own morning thoughts. She wondered what about: the play? Their holiday? The friends and relations they'd left behind for a week? It was funny, thinking about them all thinking. But there couldn't be a thought amongst them as dramatic and as strong as Patsy's. The thought of Margate getting slowly nearer. With one-night stops at Steeple Stones and Herne Bay, she was three days away from Mrs Broadley. . . .

She would take her in, wouldn't she? She would be allowed to keep her? Well, anyway, there were enough kids at school who lived with their grans, or some auntie or other. It was always happening, so why not for her? And Mrs Broadley was as good as anyone's gran. Better. Yeah, she'd fix it up somehow, of course she would. Nothing much had ever stopped Mrs Broadley from doing what she wanted, as far as Patsy could remember.

'Penny for your thoughts?'

'Eh?'

'You seemed miles away,' Pete said.

'Oh. Oh yeah. . . ?' Then she smiled at him, and leant on her elbow, resting her head sideways; the picture of contentment.

Kenny had woken to another day of being fat, and he turned his face from the light for five more minutes. It was Saturday, and there'd be no keeping out of everybody's way today. Week-ends were free-for-all outside, when none of the kids had to be in school; so there was no escaping the catcalls if he went out of the flat. And indoors wasn't much better either.

That was Kenny's first, regular, depressing Saturday thought. And as he came to today, Kenny had another. Patsy. Well, not Patsy herself, he realized, but what she'd done: because what she'd done had only made his position seem worse. See, she *could* get away. Her family was her problem, and Patsy could lose them. Well, she had lost them, getting away on that boat. But for him ... all right, he had a family problem, too, but that wasn't the big one. The big one was him; and he knew there was no way he would ever get away from being what he was. Even with all the doctors' pills and the diet sheets, he'd always be the same, he knew that. They'd as good as told him. No, it would take longer, his solution: years and years longer: the time it took to grow older and build up his strength: till people would be too afraid to call him anything but Ken, or Mr Granger. . . .

He lay there, facing the wall, and pressed his palms flat against one another, pushing, creating a tension in his muscles. He thought about this a lot, and worked at it. It might be a long job, but he was going to succeed, he was determined about that. Because even in bed you could build up the muscles in your arms: and in bed it was secret, and you didn't get so out of breath.

He closed his eyes again and pressed, like someone fervently praying for something. . . .

Eddie Green had not slept well: and Sylvia Green had not slept at all. It was as if there had been hope while there had been daylight; but darkness had brought with it a desperate anxiety instead of worry; and now the new day was only a cheat. People usually woke from a nightmare with relief: but there was no relief this morning.

Eddie Green had been out late, coming back to no further news: and after half an hour of trying to comfort Sylvia with all the wrong words he'd turned in. 'Don't you worry Sylv., I'll be up and out early,' he'd promised. ' 'Undred to one she's gone in with some friends of 'er's—some kid's mother thinking she's asked us if she can stay the night. She'll come crawling back in the morning, you see if I ain't right. . . .' But she wasn't back, and with the police keeping ominously quiet, breakfast was like the first meal after a death.

Jason kept his mother's hands busy, but not her mind, and she broke down when it came to passing Patsy's empty place with the cornflakes.

'Oh, come on,' Eddie Green said. But she shrugged him off, although he hadn't actually reached out a hand.

The doorbell rang, sudden and loud. Sylvia was there before the finger was off the button.

It was Detective Sergeant Harris, and he hadn't slept either.

'It's all right, love, it's not bad news. No news is good news at this stage of the game.'

Sylvia looked at the policewoman who was with him, as fresh and neat as an air hostess. She searched her face for some clue: but there was nothing given away with the mild smile.

Sergeant Harris walked through the hallway into the living-room. 'Well, we've ruled out that simple fellow: which is good, because it more or less rules out foul play. It's odds-on she came here *after* she'd been talking to him—going by the fact that she had her cardigan on when she was seen with him, and she didn't have it on when she came home. He's a bit vague about it, going on about bare arms and waving to him—but she could have rolled them up in the heat.

'Anyway, from what you've said, and the fat boy downstairs, it's fairly certain you saw her safe and well after he'd finished talking to her. So now we're working on the assumption that she's gone off on her own somewhere.'

The policeman's tired eyes regarded Patsy's mother. 'Sorry to ask this, Mrs Green, but was she upset over anything? She hadn't had a rollicking off one of you, had she? Only, everything seems to have been all right at the school. . . .'

55

Sylvia Green looked at Eddie: but she pursed her lips together, a moment's indecision.

But Eddie Green was suddenly defiant. 'I don't mind telling yer,' he said. 'I give 'er a clout, if that's what you mean. An' she deserved it. An' I'm not the first to 'ave done that to a kid, I know. God knows where we'd be if we couldn't give our kids a clout when they play up. . . .'

'Yes, you're very likely right. We're not reading too much into it: but you know how kids get upset sometimes: then they go off and do something silly, like this. . . .'

For a split second Eddie Green was quiet, and the edge had gone out of his eye. But only Harris saw it.

'Well, I wouldn't mind,' the little man went on, 'but I'd just give 'er permission to go on one of them school trip things after the 'oliday. Pay out again. That's what she come 'ome for, the permission. But it's never enough, what you do for 'em. It was a bit different when I was a kid. . . .'

His words fell into an unsympathetic silence; but before he could start justifying himself again the policewoman turned to Sylvia. 'Mrs Green, can you and I check on her clothes? See if anything's gone—pants or pyjamas, or anything like that?'

'And we'll need a good photograph,' Sergeant Harris told Eddie Green. 'Something recent for the papers, in case it gets to that. School photographs are usually pretty good. . . .'

Eddie Green nodded, and then looked lost, as if he didn't know where to begin to look for a photograph of Patsy. He pulled the sideboard drawer, but before his hand got in it, Sylvia screamed from Patsy's bedroom.

'She 'as!' Sylvia was in the doorway and sobbing across the room at him. 'She's taken pyjamas . . . and pants . . . and socks!' She could hardly force the words out in her anger. 'See what you've done? She's not just gone to no friends at all! She's gone off!' It looked as if she might run over and hit him, or pick up something to throw; but she stretched herself, tense and rigid, and stayed clutching at the door. 'You've done this!'

Jason screeched. Eddie Green had gone the white of death,

his expression contorted by this display of public anger, and ingratitude.

'All right, all right, don't blame yourselves. That won't do us any good. Just get us that picture and we can ask the press office to put out for her in the evening papers. Patricia *Bligh*, isn't it? Her name's *Bligh*, is that right?'

'Yes, that's her name,' Sylvia sobbed. 'My name.' Her eyes were fixed on Eddie Green. 'And there ain't no photograph, because he'd never waste his money on 'em! I've only got the baby ones I had took. They're no good, are they?'

'No, love, not a lot. They tend to mislead. . . .'

The policeman pretended to write something down, while the policewoman kept her eyes on Eddie Green. Sylvia stayed rigid.

The first to move was Eddie Green. He found his shoes and put them on. 'Well, I'm going out for a bit,' he said. ' 'Ave a look around. . . .'

Kenny was still beneath his sheet. There was nothing in the world to pull him out. With no wish to go anywhere, there was certainly nothing for him on a Saturday at home. Indoors when his father was around was a bad place to be. In the small flat Kenny always seemed to put himself in the wrong place— in a doorway when his father was coming through, behind the table when his father wanted to get there, in the bathroom two minutes before the door was rattled. It was a continual game of 'Sorry', with Kenny forever in the space his father was landing on.

'Don't stand in doorways, Kenny,' or just, 'Ttt!' was about the extent of the conversation, until at last, at half-past twelve on Saturdays, the man went off to his solitary sports. So Kenny tried to lie in bed for as long as he could, and then stay in his bedroom till it was almost time for his father to go. He never knew where he went, whether it was to a football match, or cricket, or bowling; he never talked about it; and Kenny never asked. On Sunday he went out fishing, off early and back late; and though there never seemed to be any result in which the others shared—there was certainly never a fish—Sunday wasn't so bad.

But Kenny dreaded Saturdays. No room he was in was ever big enough.

'Kenny, love. . . .'

Oh, no. She was in one of her pathetic moods again; she kept coming into the bedroom and stifling him with her closeness.

'Kenny, do you reckon little Patsy from upstairs is home yet? Mummy hasn't slept a wink, thinking. . . .'

'I dunno, do I?'

He spread himself wide under the sheet. He'd be all right as long as she didn't sit on the bed and pin him down with the bedclothes.

'That boat wasn't there no more, was it?'

Kenny squinted up at her. Was she trying to be a bit clever?

'Only Mummy was thinking, Kenny: do they know about that boat, upstairs?'

'Oh, yeah, I think so.' She'd better believe it; he didn't want to land himself in any deeper over Patsy's boat.

'Well, how's that, love? How would they know? You haven't seen them to tell, have you? Not since that lady policeman came. . . .' She sat down on the bed—he knew it had been coming—and she mooned her face over his. 'Daddy knows, Kenny. They're all talking about Patsy in the block, and Daddy knows. I told him about the boat you saw, out of interest, and he says you've definitely got to tell them. . . .'

Kenny tried to twist aside in the bed, but with her weight on the clothes he could only shift his head.

'He doesn't know about you missing school; he didn't put two and two together, not the way I told him—we'll keep that our little secret and our little promise—but he definitely says it's your *duty* to make sure they know about everything you saw, Kenny. So if you did see a boat, you've got to go up and tell them.'

58

Kenny grunted. This was bad news. And he could imagine how much interest his old man had really taken. Just enough to shut her up when she kept going on about it.

'Yes, Mummy thinks the first thing you've got to do today, Kenny, is go up and see if she's come back. And if she hasn't you can tell Patsy's mother about it. Eh? I think so. And boats have little names, don't they, Kenny? What was it called, this one? Can you remember?'

'No.' And that was the truth. He could picture the long, flat, shape of it in the creek, the new-looking, blue paint with the sun flashing on it, and he could still see Patsy waving good-bye to the barmy bloke on the bank; but he couldn't remember seeing any name. Not that he'd say if he could.

'Anyhow, what you did see is a start. Now come on, Kenny love, time for up and we'll go and see Mrs Green.' She began to move, and then she stopped, to find a little lavender handkerchief from somewhere private down inside. 'Oh, she must be feeling terrible, if that little girl hasn't been found....'

At last she took her weight off Kenny's bed and opened his curtains as wide as they would go. God! thought Kenny, she's really itching to get upstairs and put her nose in. He couldn't remember seeing her act with so much purpose. He got up; but he didn't hurry. After being stupid enough to mention the boat in the first place, the least he could do for Patsy now was take his time in telling her mum about it....

'Oh!' When they got up there Mrs Green was red-eyed, and clearly disappointed that the ring at the bell wasn't some more definite news of Patsy. 'Yes?'

'You remember me, love—Mrs Granger from the next landing down. Kenny's mother....' She stubbed a hand at Kenny as if he were the prize in some competition.

'Oh, yes.' Sylvia Green didn't ask them in; but her eyebrows lifted a little.

'Well, love ... er, she's not...?'

Sylvia shook her head and closed the door a noticeable centimetre.

'Well, Kenny's remembered something he saw, might be important. Go on, you tell Mrs Green, Kenny. . . .' She smiled, sweetly; but kept her eyes sad.

Kenny said his piece like a recitation: which it was—something carefully worked out to say. Not too much; just the fact that he had seen a boat there, around the time Patsy had been about. He kept his description of the boat to a minimum, just mentioning its colour, and its size. When he'd finished he shrugged his shoulders. It couldn't be important, he tried to imply.

Mrs Green listened carefully, and agreed with him that it had gone, later, by the time she'd got there. For a moment he thought he'd succeeded: he'd got away with satisfying his mother without arousing any undue interest from Mrs Green. But he was disappointed. Her reaction was much too interested by half.

'Mrs Granger, can your boy come with me down the police station, please? They've got to know about this.' Without waiting for an answer she disappeared indoors, to return a moment later gripping Jason by the hand. 'Mr Green's gone out for a look around. So Mrs Granger, if you wanna help, will you have Jason till I get back? I'll be quicker without him. He'll come with you. And he'll be good, won't you, Jason?'

In the sweeping forward movement, though, Jason took a step back. 'Fat lady!' he said. 'Fat boy! Fat lady!'

'You come with Auntie Maureen, love,' Mrs Granger said, grasping him firmly in her small-fingered hand. 'There's a good Jason. Good boy. Here, I've got some sweeties in my cupboard.' It was as if she hadn't heard a word he'd said in protest.

Mrs Green hurried along the landing. Kenny shuffled to keep up with her. But his scowl showed everyone that he wasn't happy: not about what he was doing, and not about what the kid had said. His stupid mother might not have heard, but he most certainly had. This kid could hardly speak, and he was saying that. Wouldn't it ever change? he thought.

Eddie Green wasn't much of a drinker, but at twelve o'clock he dived through the dark doors of the Rose. Outside, the sun on the awnings had given the Cut a Caribbean flavour, and with all those exotic shirts and rasta hair styles, and long, cool dresses floating by, Deptford seemed like carnival. But not for Eddie Green. Nobody much had even understood what he was on about with his questions about a girl and a blue boat, and most of the street-traders had let him see that they really thought he was only after a soft touch. Sweating now, after another two hours of it, he widened his eyes in the anonymous gloom of the public bar and ran his tongue over his top lip.

Already the bar was busy; but as his beer was being poured he asked the barman his question.

'A kid in our flats says there was a big boat in the creek yesterday. Along behind Jordan's works. Didn't see anything of 'em, did you?' The beer frothed heavily to the top of the glass.

'Yeah.' The barman looked at him. 'Funny lot, wasn't they?' He turned, rang up the till, and moved along the bar to serve someone else.

Eddie sipped. His face gave nothing away. 'Didn't say who they was, did they?' he asked when the man came back to pour him a second.

'No. But like I said, they was a funny lot. A bit la-di-da. Not from round here. Going down the coast somewhere. Down Kent, Sheerness way.' He spoke to the glass. 'Typical tourists! I 'ad to get a bit strong when one of 'em tried to walk an ashtray off. Why, do you know 'em, do you?'

'No! Only . . .' he leant over the glass, witholding his money till he'd said what he wanted . . . 'only my girl's done a bunk. An' you know, I wondered if she might've. . . .'

'How old?'

'Eleven, twelve, thirteen, something like that. . . .'

The barman looked at him, hard. 'No, mate. The only girl was about twenty. Bit of all right, an' all. Three men, all had a few drinks, big box of groceries, and the girl. But they didn't have no kid with 'em. Sorry, mate.'

'Yeah. Sheerness, did you say?'

'That way. That's what one of 'em was on about. . . .' And he moved away as his eye was caught further along the bar.

Eddie Green drank up and went straight home.

Sylvia jumped on the news. 'We ain't sitting on this!' she said. 'I tell you. When I was out last night, did I see one bloody policeman going round? There wasn't no one doing nothing, not even a car going up and down the streets. No, mate, if we're gonna find her we're gonna 'ave to go out and find her ourselves. Now at least we know where to start. . . .'

Within minutes she was down at Kenny's door.

'He *can* go, can't he, Mrs Granger? He saw the boat. He knows what it looks like. And there'll be hundreds of boats down the coast, weather like this. Eddie'll look after him. I'll draw some money out. They'll be all right for cash.'

'Well, yes, love, of course, that'll be all right with Kenny. . . .'

'They can get straight down there. Catch a train and have a good look round Sheerness. . . .'

'We'll do anything to help, love, you know that. . . .'

'I *know* that's what she's done. Hidden herself on it, I bet, while the people was in that pub. . . .'

'We're only too glad to help, love. Oh, what you must be going through. . . . Kenny's got good eyes. And he'll be a very good boy for Mr Green, won't you, Kenny? And Mr Green can ring through to me, on our 'phone, if he likes. Kenny knows the number. You know Daddy's number, don't you, Kenny?'

Kenny's sullen nod was lost in his neck. He clenched his fists. He wasn't meant to be pushed around like this. But before he knew it, he found himself standing on Deptford station, back to back with the man, waiting in silence for the next train which would connect with the Kent coast.

It had all happened so suddenly. And it was all getting right out of hand.

6

These were just as bad as train timetables, Jenny said, unfolding the Ordnance Survey map for Patsy. They were always crammed with masses of detail, and you had to be really desperate to make it worth your while bothering with them. 'It's quicker to ask,' she advised, 'and look helpless!'

They were in the cabin on their own, preferring shade to the unremitting sun on their fair skins. Patsy had found the map in a side panel and had chosen her moment to ask innocently about the distances along the Thanet Way between Steeple Stones, Herne Bay, and Margate.

'Oh, lordy, these are all in kilometres as well, now: but, look, you can see here. . . .' Jenny twisted and turned the map against the folds, fattening it up like yesterday's newspaper. 'Steeple Stones to Herne Bay's about five miles, and Margate's another . . . what, ten miles further on? Or is that kilometres? Anyway, they're not very far apart, all round this same bit of coast. Not far by sea, and not far by land. But who cares about Margate yet, my girl? It's luxury all the way in the *Dame Sybil*, or don't you think so?'

'Yeah.' Patsy nodded eagerly. God, she'd better not make them think she was getting fed up—or there was anything special about Margate: not till the time was right to clear off.

She tried to visualize a mile. Eddie Green always complained that from home to the Labour was a mile there and back. That was fifteen times that to get along the red road on the map, if everything went wrong and she had to go from here.

'And now what's puzzling you, young lady? Come back, come back!'

Patsy laughed, like the good little actress they kept telling her she was. She stretched her legs and coiled up again with an interested frown.

'That's a funny old name, i'n it? *Dame* what-was-it?'

'*Dame Sybil*. Theatrical, lovey. Dame Sybil Thorndike, a very famous actress. Joe was a fan.'

'Oh, yeah?' But her eyes were back on the map, drawn by the little pink bars of back streets behind Margate. One of those was the one, she thought.

'Five years old, this map. See, I'm not stupid after all. And I'm beginning to sort out some sense from all these signs and symbols: church with a steeple, church without a steeple; metalled road, unmetalled road. I suppose it all falls into place after a while, if you stick at it.'

'Yeah.' The metalled road sounded all right. Margate. Streets paved with gold, as far as she was concerned.

'Oh, you are a bit quiet, lovey. Not homesick, are you? Not missing your Jason, and Mum and Dad? Because if you are, darling, you've only got to say the word. I'll take you home on the train, we decided that....'

'No! No—I'm great!'

'Good.' Jenny flashed a smile at her. She gave her a squeeze, and laughed. They both laughed, and they drank an ice-cold Coke between them to seal their contentment.

Two hours further on and Steeple Stones sounded out a welcome. Even in the calm, the slightest breeze off the water was rattling the sail lines against the metal masts with a chattering like applause. Bob, his face freckled by the sun and his shoulders scorched across, leapt off the side and secured the *Dame Sybil*'s prow to a bollard, while Pete saw to the stern. There was a sudden flurry of movement. Even Ruth, glistening brown, got up from her spread towel. They had arrived, and after the unhurried pleasure of the journey in that exceptional weather, they were going to have to get on with what they'd come for.

They'd done all the arranging well, Patsy thought. From

65

among the shimmering dots of colour that were people on the shingle beach a couple in shorts and T-shirts waved and approached.

'Great timing, Joe,' called the man.

'Of course. I know my tides!'

'Well you're all right here. I've seen the harbour master. And Dennis arrived with the skip about half-an-hour ago. Buy him a drink, Peter, he says the M2 was murder!'

Jenny explained for Patsy. 'Ruth's brother, Dennis. He brought the clothes and the props down by road in his van.'

'Oh.' Patsy tried not to frown. That didn't sound very clever. Every tossed-out bit of news had to be reckoned against her own plans. That meant that apart from the train, there was a van they could bung her off home in, if she got found out.

She felt all churned up inside. She didn't like these links with London.

'Come on, then, Patsy, let's show you the Theatre Royal.' Patsy's frown this time was nicely puzzled. 'The church hall. But don't call it that; they're very proud of it. It's really a very nice little theatre.'

Patsy didn't know what she expected to see—she didn't care a lot; after all, it was *their* game she was playing, for the time being; but from the outside it certainly didn't look anything very grand. The red brick building was tucked in the middle of a row of small houses, with an alley's width to spare on either side: and although it said, 'Steeple Stones Little Theatre' in faded fluorescent paint, it was definitely a church hall, there was no disguising that. But if the outside was very ordinary, once through the double doors of the small foyer, the soft smell of plush seats and the first darkened glimpse of closed stage curtains stabbed her with a nervous excitement, deep in the pit of the stomach.

God! It was a bit real! She hoped she'd be all right after all her showing off.

SPECIAL ATTRACTION

The Upper Thames Players

IN

A HAPPY RELEASE

A comedy thriller by

Harry Powell

read a placard on a small easel in the doorway. Jenny sounded
a fanfare as she sidled past it, and Patsy smiled nervously. It
wasn't quite like having her name read out on the Breakfast
Show; but it was getting close.

Not that she wanted anything like that—not this week-end!

The local man had seen her looking, and probably seen her
smile. 'We'll duplicate a little slip for the programme,' he
offered. 'We didn't think there'd be a Tracey—and people
like to know who's who....'

'No! It don't matter.' Who wanted this lot knowing she was
Patsy Bligh? *Someone* would be looking for her, wouldn't they?

'Oh, you must have your name in the programme, lovey.'
Jenny was very positive. 'Green, isn't it? Patsy Green?'

Patsy shrugged, pretending to give in gracefully. 'Yeah,'
she said. She'd settle for that. Eddie's name on the letter.
Well, that was all right, because nobody at home knew her as
Patsy Green.

'Right,' said the man. 'So be it. Pete, I think Dennis is
waiting round the back for a hand with the skip. If you help
him I'll get the tabs open and start sorting out the lights....'

The next two hours should have passed like five minutes. It
was all new to Patsy, all very professional and important, like
being in a television show, or a film. Lights were set up, props
were laid out, and costumes were hung on long rails in the
mirror-lined dressing-room. Everybody seemed to enjoy
shouting directions in loud, confident voices; and they were all
in their element, working hard at what made them happy. Joe

seemed to revel in it more than anyone. He was the centre, the man with two circles of friends there, and this was really his day. He put Patsy in mind of a kid at school with a birthday, going round in the best of moods; and for herself—miles away from Eddie Green—as well as for the infectious Joe, she should have felt very happy.

But that couldn't happen. Not for Patsy Bligh, she thought bitterly. Something always had to spoil things for her. And after only half-an-hour in the little theatre, Dennis and his *London Evening News* turned Patsy's Saturday into a nightmare afternoon.

She saw it as soon as he'd flopped it, tired and creased, out of his zip-front on to one of the seats in the front row. Luckily it was folded with the stop-press facing up, or Patsy, sitting there sorting out Jenny's make-up box, wouldn't have been the first to see what it said.

LONDON GIRL MISSING

. . . It wasn't, was it? But Patsy was aware of her name down there in the faint print before she actually read it. Holding her breath she searched for it, and seeing it—with a sudden tightness drawn across her chest—she read the three lines from the top. 'Eleven-year-old London schoolgirl, four feet nine, fair-haired, wearing pink silk dress, missing from home in Harding Court, Deptford, since yesterday. Police believe missing girl Patricia Bligh ran away from home after a quarrel.' The rest of the column, right down the side of the paper, was blank: there was no more late news, not even a racing result. Just her bit, and all that space to make it stand out.

Patsy stared at it without touching the newspaper, her mind trying to reject what her eyes were telling her. *Was* that her name there? In the paper, just the way you read about everybody else? No doubt. It was her name, and it was her. Good God! They weren't half trying hard to catch her.

But the burning question was, had Dennis read it? Was he

going to toss it all anyhow into the talk during the evening? And if he did, would they tie it in with her? She tried to console herself a bit. There wasn't any photograph, was there? And they hadn't used the name they knew her by down here. All the same, there was plenty to point the finger her way. *There was the address for a start.*

Patsy went on looking at the paper as if it were burning hot. She knew it would have seemed quite natural for her to pick it up and glance at it, in between what she was doing, sorting out the make-up sticks; but somehow it seemed too inflammable for that. No one was actually looking, but it was as if the whole world could see her every move. Like one of Jason's toys, she daren't put her hand out towards it in case there was a loud and sudden scream. So she sat there next to it in a turmoil of what-to-do.

If she did touch it, should she stuff the whole paper out of sight? Or just get rid of that back page? The trouble was, people missed front and back pages where they didn't miss the insides. Eddie Green landed out often enough if she used the front and back for Jason's budgie.

Patsy's face felt as cold as ice, even to her own touch: and a hungry feeling that wasn't hunger filled her inside.

What the hell was she going to do then? Get up and walk out of the theatre and get off on the road to Margate? That wasn't a bad idea. Except it was getting on, and she'd stand out like a sore thumb walking along that road in the evening.

What a rotten bloody trick! She hadn't thought about this sort of thing happening when she'd jumped on the boat, had she? She'd thought it'd be easy, once she was on that river. Walk on and walk off to Mrs Broadley. But with the police and the papers she didn't stand much chance at all; she could see that, all of a sudden. Once she got to Mrs Broadley it'd be all right; it'd be in her hands, and she'd get things sorted out; do it proper and make it all official. But if she never got that far, she didn't stand a chance in hell. . . .

Jenny stepped out of a circle of light on the stage and

jumped down in front of her. Patsy suddenly felt paralysed—
like being found quickly covering up her bed by Eddie Green.
Was Jenny going to see it? All Patsy could do was sit there and
wait, see what happened. There was nothing in the world she
could do for herself. The paper was just there, and Jenny was
just there; and everything was out of her hands.

'Not bored are you, lovey? We'll do some rehearsing in a
little while.'

'No.' *Bored?* Patsy found it hard to get enough breath to
speak. But she forced herself on. 'I done most of this sorting of
the make-up. I never knew there was all these different
colours. All these reds. . . .' It was a trick she'd learned with
Eddie Green: start talking about something—anything—and
there was just a chance you'd take their mind off it. 'I've put
'em all together, and the others, in their colours. . . .'

'God, what you accumulate! I never knew. Hey, that's an
unusual red. Where on earth did I pick that up?' Jenny's
attention was on the top tray of the make-up box now. Patsy
shifted nervously on the plush seat. A second-by-second
game, this was: and she was years from winning yet.

'It's a bit lighter than I usually wear.' Jenny picked out the
narrow stick and stroked it on the back of her hand, looking
critically at the lines of colour she'd drawn. 'It's rather
unusual, though, isn't it? Nice for sunny days. . . .' Someone
had put the stage lights full on, and the spill into the front
stalls was lighting up her striped hand, and her face. She
picked up a hand mirror and worked the colour on to her
stretched lips.

Still there was nothing Patsy could do but just sit and watch
her. And notice from the corner of her eye how white the
newspaper glared in the lights.

'What do you think, lovey? A bit too light for my
skin?'

Deep breath. 'No.' Another breath. 'It's all right.' Patsy
was a long way away from lipstick.

'Too shiny, though. Eh?' Jenny lifted the top tray of the

make-up box. 'Makes me look like a tart. Blot it down ... tissues. ...'

She rummaged, but there were none in there. Then it happened. Before Patsy even knew she'd thought about it, she turned and tore the stop-press column down the *Evening News*, and calmly handed the white strip to Jenny to use as a tissue. Patsy's bit was there in Jenny's hand. 'Here y'are, that's clean. Not much printing on that.'

'Ta, lovey.' Jenny folded the paper and kissed it, and screwed it to toss into a box of lamps. 'Oh, yes, that's better. You know, I quite fancy this colour. ...'

Patsy stared, and trembled a smile; and a few moments later when Jenny went back to standing under a light for Pete, she sat back in her front seat, as if she were at the pictures. She'd done it. The danger had passed. For a bit, anyhow. Well, for as long as everyone else kept clear of newspapers, she reckoned. And as she relaxed she gradually began to feel pleased with herself at the quick action she'd taken. Clever, it had been: definitely. Perhaps if she could keep on her toes the same as that for the next couple of days she might just make it after all, she told herself.

'Patsy!'

Pete wanted her up on the stage with Ruth and Bob, to walk her through the scene—show her where to stand when she came in, which spotlight to find with her face, and where to move as she said her words. He didn't want acting, he said.

'O.K.' He was very matter-of-fact when they'd finished. 'Give me a bit less amber in number two spot, Dennis. They must see the girl's face. ...'

There was a lot of coming and going, then; and Patsy came and went like a professional.

'All right, sweetheart?' In one of the hundred black-outs Joe suddenly squeezed the breath out of Patsy with a strong arm round her waist. He tucked her under it and with the box of lights under the other he strode across to the pass door backstage. Patsy pummelled and kicked: but she was laughing, and she didn't go too hard. It had been a long time since anyone had romped with her like this.

'Yeah, I'm all right,' she said, when she was put down. 'Thanks.'

And she was, now. The newspaper business was behind her for the moment, and she was beginning to enjoy all this acting and romping and attention. While at the back of her mind all the time was the thought that when this was over in a couple of days she was going back to Mrs Broadley. Keep thinking that, she seemed to be saying; the dream's well on its way to coming true.

' 'Scuse!' she said to Joe as she pushed past him to go back to her plush seat at the front. 'I don't want to miss nothing. . . .'

From the way Eddie Green was going on, this journey was going to turn out very different to all the telly adverts you saw, Kenny thought: those things where people just hopped on trains and got where they were going, all cool and calm, arriving hours in front of all the swearing motorists. No, this was going to be a long, slow, business, with two changes before they got to Sheerness—and Eddie was really winding himself up as he walked in circles on the narrow platform.

'It's a bloody driver's world,' he spat at the rails, 'and don't you believe otherwise. Door to door, 'op in the car and down the A2, no trouble. Down there in an hour. Different to this! They can shove this for a lark! Change at Rochester, change at Sittingbourne! Thank you very much! It'll be five o'clock before we even get to Sheerness, let alone start looking around for boats. You can stuff the railways!

'And as for that little madam!' he spat the next time round. 'Just wait till I catch up with 'er. . . .' He looked at Kenny as if it were all his fault, and Kenny—although he tried to kid himself he was above caring what Eddie Green thought—was relieved when at last the slow green caterpillar of a train came round the bend into the station.

Not that getting moving helped much. He didn't want to go anywhere with that short temper—and he could sense the man's impatience physically, like a push in the back, as he sweated up the steep steps to the carriage.

'All right, I'll sit facing,' Eddie Green said. 'See where we are.'

Kenny changed and sat with his back to the way they were going. It wasn't which way he faced that he minded. It was the sitting. He always felt fatter sitting down than he did standing up. His thighs spread out like levelling dough and his feet dangled wide apart; his stomach sank and his arms stuck out at his sides as if they'd been stitched on like a fat rag doll's. There couldn't be any crossing of his legs, no folding of his arms, no twisting of his head. When you were fat like he was you just sat; you hardly moved till you heaved yourself up to go. It was like being left in a wheelchair.

Eddie Green looked at him, as if he were noticing him for the first time. 'Christ,' he said at last, 'you need a crash diet, you do. Can't your mum keep you off the chips?'

Kenny wanted to ignore the man: but sitting staring at one another the way they were made that difficult; and with them being teamed up together all day he didn't want a bad start.

'No. It's not that. It don't seem to make no difference what I eat. . . .'

'No? Well, it should, son. If you was my boy I'd make a difference, I tell you. For your own good. . . .'

Kenny shrugged. Oh, yeah? he thought. Who was he kidding? He wouldn't care any more about him than he did about Patsy. And Kenny knew how he treated her. Funny how different some people pretended to be, outside their flats. His own old man was probably like this, he thought. Completely different to strangers when he went out.

To Kenny's relief, things went quiet for a while, and it seemed as if Eddie Green had calmed down a bit now they were moving. Kenny relaxed slightly and watched him light a fat cigarette, sitting there with his bullet head sideways on the oily rest, staring out at the rows of small back gardens. While the man's beady eyes flickered about, Kenny took him all in: the chequered shirt, the stiff jeans, the high-heeled shoes, and the hard, bony hands. Patsy was dead right. He wouldn't trust Eddie Green any further than he could throw him. He looked a right spiteful piece of work.

The train swayed on. Greenwich, Maze Hill, tunnels and cuttings and squealing stops, Woolwich Arsenal, the grey moon-city of Thamesmead, the marshes, and the long tunnel to Strood, like a journey in the night. Then the bright, winding thread of the Medway, and Rochester Castle in the sun, till the depressing slam of doors and 'All change here for the Kent coast' sounded out. Four cigarette ends flattened to the floor, pins and needles in Kenny's dangling limbs, and not a single word in the carriage since Dartford.

'Come on. Out!' said Eddie Green. 'Look sharp, we've only got three quarters of a bloody hour to wait here....'

Again, the station platform was narrow, and again the little man started his circling: round and round, muttering, and driving people away.

From where he was on the raised platform Kenny could see over the roofs to a narrow reach of the Medway, where the week-end sailors were moving slowly on the calm water. A Thames barge with heavy red sails was progressing down river on the ebbing tide, and away from London there was a cool air of contentment in the heat. Lucky Patsy! Kenny thought: enjoying all that cool on her boat somewhere: no hot, sore legs for her, no sweating on some wild-goose chase.

A cool idea suddenly struck him. Why not put the tin lid on it now? How about pretending he thought he could see the boat from here; one of those over there? Get themselves down to the river to find it, miss the train they were waiting for, and go back home? He'd make sure he didn't get brought back again, not if he was really vague about the boat ... and it would help to make him feel a bit better inside about saying as much as he had....

76

'Now you just tell me why she done it!'

Kenny jumped. He hadn't seen Eddie Green come up to him, cut suddenly across his paced circle.

'Because I don't see it. She's got a good 'ome, 'er own room and everything, an' she don't want for nothing. But she ups and goes off like some moody little madam. Now you just tell me the answer, 'cos I'm damned if I know it!'

Kenny looked blank and shook his head. He shrugged, too.

'Just wait till I bloody catch 'er, that's all!'

Eddie Green looked so fierce that Kenny immediately abandoned any idea of trying to fool him just yet. He might happen not to see the boat down at Sheerness, but he was damned if he was risking the man's temper by mucking him about before he had to.

'No, 'er mother's spoilt 'er, that's Madam's trouble. Been too easy with 'er. Both of us. Not like my old man with me. Knew where I stood, I did. No silly nonsense with 'im. Do this, do that, an' if you didn't do what you was told you got what-for.'

Kenny had to stand and listen. There was nothing else he could do: but he wished to God the man would start going round in his circles again.

'Yeah, my old man.... It's funny 'ow your mind goes back.' The man stood and stared into the distance, over the roof tops towards the high banks which sloped over Chatham. His voice had changed. It had lost its edge, somehow, like someone with a cold. 'Not far from 'ere, as it 'appens.'

Without any warning the wiry figure spun and cursed at the gleaming lines. 'Come on, come on, where's that bloody train?'

Kenny frowned. Strange, that had been. Just for a moment, for a couple of sentences, he'd had a glimpse of someone else.

7

Being away from her mum was a treat, Patsy thought: not the same sort of treat as being away from Eddie Green was; but simply the pleasure of doing things because she wanted to, not because she was forced. Like, at home she had to wash up, run down the shops, 'pull her weight'; while with these people here what she did to help was done off her own bat—and they thanked her for it. That made a real change. They made a great big fuss of her helping to lay the table for tea in the theatre entrance hall; and as she passed the mugs round she kept getting those big, beaming thank-you's from everyone as if she was doing them all the biggest favour in the world.

And then, on top of that, just for a while today she had that secure feeling that everything wasn't going to blow up in her face any minute. She felt safe from being found out, somehow; almost as if here, with all the make-believe, they'd shut the door on the real world outside; and there just didn't seem much chance of anyone coming in with another evening paper—or reading it, even if they did. Once he'd dumped his, Dennis hadn't given it another thought. No, they were all too wrapped up in what they were doing on the stage.

The lights were all set up, the scenery flats were secure, and the doors of the stage living-room opened properly. After tea they were going to run through the whole thing: a full-scale dress rehearsal. Gradually, the nervous cigarettes were being lit up, the conversation was becoming louder. Eventually, Pete called them to order, and they drifted into the dressing-room behind the stage to get made-up. Now there were soft mutterings of lines, a few jokes, but their concentration was really on themselves in the mirrors—the girls in their wraps at the far end, the men with towels in their collars near the door; and for fifteen minutes they were too bound up in their appearances to pay much attention to anyone else. It put Patsy in mind of her mum going out to work in the old Margate days—at bedtime, when whatever she had to say she came next in line behind Sylvia's reflection—and now she didn't like it much either, till Jenny, finished first, sat her up in her place and started putting on a light liquid foundation with a pad of cotton wool.

'We won't overdo it, lovey; just a touch of colour so you won't look like a ghost under the lights....' Grey-blue eye shadow, a faint smear off Jenny's little finger—a careful blue line under the rim of each eye, and deep orange lips.

'There, that'll look natural, you see—not made-up at all.'

There was no kissing a bit of paper this time: just careful pressing with a powder pad: a few strokes with Jenny's hair brush and Patsy was swung round to look at herself in the mirror.

Hey, not bad! In fact, a bit near the mark! Left side, right side, head back and looking sultry down her nose, showing her white teeth. It wouldn't only be Mary McArthy who had the Deptford Sec. boys tripping over their bags if they could see this Patsy here....

Jenny gave her a thumbs-up before disappearing behind a curtain to get changed. Everybody started talking at once, chairs were scraped back, and the cast started moving about in a haze of fine powder and hair spray.

Suddenly, Patsy's shoulders were gripped from behind. A squeeze from Joe. Contact that wasn't a smack was rare. 'Well, there's a treat!' he said. 'The beautiful Miss Bligh! Too grown-up to be called Patsy now!'

She laughed at Joe in the mirror. Yeah, she wasn't bad! And that was nice for someone to say so. Whoever would have praised her before, except Mrs Broadley? They were terrific people, these. Joe smiled back at her, and winked. He looked a bit strange, lop-sided, seen through a mirror; but when Patsy swung back to him he was his old, teasing self. He put his hand in his pocket and took out a coin, pressing it in her palm and folding her fingers over it. 'It's ten pence to talk to you now.' He pulled a funny face and pretended to touch his cap, before ambling back down the line with a jokey comment for everyone else.

Patsy felt ready. She had no changing to do; her own pink dress was just about right for the scene; but now the hanging-about began. All standing ready, it affected them all, even the experienced ones. Gradually, a new tension grew into the atmosphere, curling itself tight, like the tendrils of an attacking plant. It gripped them generally, and individually. It surprised Patsy. All at once her stomach seemed to be turning itself inside out. Dressed and made-up for act one, Pete muttered over a torch-lit script in the dark auditorium; while the rest of them whispered and jostled and fanned themselves in the heat of the dark wings. It was a long, tense wait. But it didn't make two ha'porth of difference, did it? Patsy tried to tell herself. With all her worries, why should doing this little bit on the stage suddenly make her feel so bad? It was horrible, the churning. Don't worry! she thought. This is nothing! If you make the biggest mess of it, it's a flea-bite compared to everything else! Then another thought struck her. Was the real worry about running away? If so, what had happened to make her feel bad again, after just feeling all right over the paper and everything? Jenny was muttering her words to herself. She couldn't think. No. Stop being stupid, it was this play. Whether she cared or not, it was a nervous time, waiting like this. She started to go over her own words again; but before she'd done her short speech for the third time, the curtains jerked closed across the empty space.

'All right,' shouted Joe. 'Ready for act one.' Like a zombie, silent and stiff, Ruth glided through the doorway on to the set. Joe crept on next to her. He said something funny, which didn't make her laugh. It was just like doing the Nativity, Patsy thought; everyone got like this, even Mrs Daulton.

Joe and Ruth stood in their positions, ready for the big argument which started the play: the row which set the scene for Joe's murder....

'Well, come on, then,' she muttered. 'My foot's gone to sl....'

Without warning, the curtains parted, drawing in cooler air and a snow of dust. The lights were full on. There was a moment's expectant silence. Nobody breathed. 'How dare you?!' The tension was suddenly relieved by Ruth and Joe bursting into the middle of their big row. It began fiercely; and was so realistic that Patsy, who hadn't seen this bit before, could only watch through narrowed eyes. The two of them stood toe to toe and just clawed at each other with words, working up to a climax where they were hurling their angry faces at one another. The poison of it held Patsy paralysed. She'd heard all this in the flats—only the words were different—and she knew how it would end; Joe would go for Ruth with his strong hands. It seemed inevitable. But at just the moment when Joe seemed unable to hold himself in check for another second, in flitted Jenny with a can of Brasso and a rag, making some stupid remark about the naughty sun on her dusty windows. Joe shook the canvas wall like an earthquake as he slammed out of the room in a temper. He flung the door closed behind him and bore down on Patsy in the darkness backstage.

She flinched.

'All right, darling?' he said, putting his arm round her waist and squeezing her hard. 'And how do you like being an actress? Suit you, this life, does it?'

'Yeah, it's all right,' she whispered. She experienced a sudden feeling of cautious relief. Funny, she thought, how these theatre people could switch on and switch off. A few seconds ago she'd have run a mile to get away from him. 'Anyhow,' she said, 'I'll tell you when I've done my bit.'

Joe felt her arm. 'Not cold are you, sweetheart? Want a

drop of the old Dutch courage?' He produced a brandy bottle from nowhere.

'No thanks! I'll get drunk!' She deliberately put on the little giggle that had to go with saying that. It was strange, this mix-up of feelings she was having with Joe. All of a sudden she didn't understand how she felt about him. But it was probably the part he was taking, she told herself. He was one person on the stage, and someone quite different back here.

Joe laughed softly and went back to his stage manager's desk, leaving Patsy to stand well back from the glassless window and watch the action through it. It was quite good, she thought. Not really like real life any more, not now the row was over: the things they were all saying were too clever and worked out for that: but what she enjoyed was the way a series of funny lines had you laughing, and then, bang! something sinister happened. It kept doing that. But through it all, what really kept her in a state of anticipation was the relentless approach of her own scene at the end of the act.

She began to follow the play in the book. Gradually, the pages to go went down from five, to three, to one, till at last, fluttering inside, it was time to tiptoe with Jenny to the closed door of the set. She tried to draw some deep breaths; but it was too late now to be able to do that.

'Come in slowly when I hold the door open: and don't forget that scared look, lovey.'

'That won't be no trouble,' Patsy muttered. 'Anyhow, keep your fingers crossed.'

In a sudden movement, Jenny knocked on the frame of the canvas door, leaving Patsy behind as she went bustling in: and twenty seconds later, Patsy found herself being ushered in to the bright lights of the open stage.

'Here goes! Good luck, girl!' she murmured in her head.

There was Bob again, but dressed as the detective in a sharp suit, all casual and full of confidence.

'"Ah, Tracey Brewer, is it?"'

' "Yes, sir." '

' "And you've seen something you want to tell us about?" '

' "Yes, sir." '

He was taking his part very well, Patsy thought; smiling like Mr Lamb when he asked you questions; shouting it out to be heard at the back, but making it seem ever so real. She kept her mind concentrating hard, ready for her speech; but what she found was that she had this extra part of her brain which kept an eye on everything else. It was quite surprising. She was Tracey, and she was Patsy, too. As Patsy, her eyes were mildly dazzled by gentle amber spotlight from somewhere out deep in the hall: while as Tracey, she knew she had something important to say to the police. It was funny, she found herself thinking, how your brain sometimes worked on different levels at once.

Jenny had gone off, to leave her alone to tell them what she'd seen out in the lane that night. Ruth was acting up well as a very scared, famous actress, showing dignity and fear, both at the same time. It was all going very well, and Patsy felt in command.

Bob spoke to her again. ' "Well, young lady, I think you'd better describe this man you saw. You never know, it could have some bearing on this unpleasant business." '

Patsy took a deep breath. ' "Yes, sir," ' she said. ' "Well, it was as dark as pitch, and I was in one 'ell of a rush to get 'ome. But I see 'im, sir, coming out the back way. You know, the little gate the milkman uses." '

' "Yes, go on." '

' "Well, 'e was about as tall as you, sir, and 'e 'ad a droopy moustache, like . . ." ' Here Patsy had to slow, as if she had suddenly realized who it had really been like . . . Pete, who was on the other side of the stage, turning his face away from the detective. ' ". . . Like one of them old-time cowboys. And 'e was wearing . . ." ' here she put a slight edge of fear into her voice, ' ". . .'e 'ad those jeans sort of trousers, and . . ." ' Now she was looking at Pete, widening her eyes. ' "And a black

83

leather jacket on top. That's what I saw, sir, before 'e ran away. . . ." ' She held the accusation in her eyes.

By now the detective had stopped writing, and while Ruth took a half step towards Patsy, as if she were about to slap her face, he turned slowly to stare at Pete, and while he stood there, and they all froze, the curtains came gently across.

It was a thrilling moment, and Patsy felt the electricity of it contracting the skin down her back.

She had never been the centre of so much dramatic attention in all her life.

There was a long, long silence. And then, no voices, but the sound of hand clapping; very, very, hard. The tip-up seats banged as the local team of helpers stood up to applaud.

'Terrific, lovey!'

'Great!' Pete bounded across the stage and crouched down before Patsy. 'Keep it just like that,' he said. 'It was perfect.' He kissed her on the forehead.

'Great!'

'Well done, darling!'

Swept up in the group's effusive congratulations Patsy's feet found it hard to stay on the ground, with all the enthusiastic words, and kisses, and squeezes, and pats on the back. And being interval time now, there was no mad rush to be on to the next thing.

'Never act with dogs and children!' Bob told the cheerful dressing-room. 'You can't win!'

Patsy, for all their overdoing it, still couldn't stop herself from smiling. Jenny toasted her with cold tea in a paper cup. There was yet another spatter of applause and a lot more noise, until Pete had to remind them that they did still have half the play to run through. While the others changed, Patsy sat on her chair and looked at herself, this little Tracey in the mirror; curling and uncurling her toes. What a peculiar lot they were, all of them, making so much of everything. She definitely wasn't used to it. Mr Lamb had twenty-nine others to look to in the class; and she never did a thing right at home.

But these were really nice, and friendly. And there was Joe, coming up behind her with a smile.

'A very good bit of acting,' he said quietly. 'I should reckon it's . . . what? . . . twenty pence to speak to Miss Bligh now. . . .'

Patsy laughed and took the money he was handing to her. And her stomach fell away as if it had been ripped out by some evil hand.

Oh, Jesus, now she knew why she'd felt so strange before. It hadn't just been nervousness about the play. It had been something else besides.

Every cell of the actress in her tried to keep her face smiling at Joe, but a numbing silence had filled her head and suddenly taken the place of all that congratulation.

The man knew, didn't he?

Eddie Green's behaviour had changed. Instead of urging the train on, swearing at delays in catching up with Patsy, he was sitting forward on the edge of his seat, squinting out in the bright heat, first on one side of the carriage, then on the other, as if he were determined not to miss a single telegraph-pole that went skimming by. Through the tunnel to Chatham, under the Lines to Gillingham, on the long country run towards Sittingbourne, all the way he swivelled at views like a two-year-old on a bus. Kenny, hot and gasping in the smoky carriage, found it disconcerting, unsettling. How could you relax in all this heat when a grown man was behaving like a little kid with worms? When you expected certain things from people, why did they have to throw you off balance by suddenly changing the way they were?

'Used to be all orchards down 'ere,' Eddie Green said, out of the blue. 'All this was orchards.' He jerked his arm. 'Cherries. All down 'ere, between the railway line and the river.' But he kept turning this way and that. He was still searching for something, and it was obvious it wasn't orchards.

Kenny made a small effort to look out. On his left he could see estates of newish-looking houses coming right up to the railway embankment; and on his right he could see the orchards, still there.

'An' this railway was different then. All steam. None of these electric rails. I used to run like 'ell across the line just before the train come—and back across 'fore something else come the other way. . . .' He lit another cigarette, puffing at it quickly. 'I never realized it was this line we was coming on.'

Kenny stared at him. Whatever the man had to say he still managed to make it sound like an accusation: but it was clear he was strongly affected by going back through where he used to live.

The train stopped at Rainham. Eddie Green sat back and blew out a long brown plume of smoke. 'Used to swim down there an' all,' he said, suddenly confidential. 'Down the bottom, past the orchards. All soft mud. A killer if you put your foot down. Used to get down there on my bike and strip off and into that river just before 'igh water. A sight better'n swimming baths, I can tell you. . . .'

Kenny was really listening now; and if he was staring, he didn't mind. This was getting interesting. Someone else who liked getting in that real water? Took a risk in the river? Was Eddie Green another proper swimmer?

And did Eddie Green know about him? All at once, Kenny had a strong urge to tell him.

'My old man would've gone barmy if 'e'd known the things I used to get up to as a kid. . . . There it is!' He made Kenny jump. 'Quick, look out there, there's another place.'

Kenny picked out what the man was pointing at; what he'd been searching for. Down by the river were three tall, green cylinders, smooth tower-like things; cement kilns or something, he thought; quite high and standing next to one another, joined together across the top by a sort of narrow gangway.

'Still there! God! 'Asn't changed since I was a kid. When I think what I used to do up there. . . .'

Kenny frowned. Eddie Green had changed the subject; and

for some unknown reason he would very much have liked to tell him about his own swimming. . . .

'Eh?'

Kenny realized he must have made some noise, when he'd thought he'd only been thinking.

'What?'

'I was just thinking: I like a swim myself. . . .'

'Oh, yeah?' Eddie Green had turned away to stare out at the slow fields.

'You know, in the river, sort of thing. . . .'

'In the river? What, the Thames? Near us?'

He'd got the man's attention back. And now he felt a bit ashamed for wanting to. 'Yeah. That's when I saw . . . things. I was having a swim then. . . .'

'Yeah? Oh. . . .' Eddie Green sat forward. He looked Kenny up and down. 'Well, you want to watch it. Different kettle of fish, the Thames is. . . .'

'I don't swallow nothing.'

'No, that's right, you don't want to. But it's the currents with the Thames. Yeah, that's interesting. I didn't know anyone 'ad the bottle to do that round our way. What's your dad say?' Eddie Green was really taking an interest.

'He don't know.'

'No?' Eddie Green thought about that. 'Like me. . . .' He sat back, and gave Kenny a long, last look before he made his head comfortable in the angle of the seat and the window and closed his eyes. Kenny settled back, too; and he felt strangely satisfied as the train swayed on to Sittingbourne.

By the time Kenny and Eddie Green got on to the Isle of Sheppey, though, things were anything but relaxed. Why couldn't someone have told him? Eddie Green started moaning. Why hadn't anyone said they should have got off at Queenborough? Why hadn't someone said that's where the small boats always moored up? Now they had to go back there from Sheerness, and there wouldn't be another train for at

least two hours. The air was foul for a few minutes; and Kenny was only grateful this poison wasn't meant for him.

'Well, we'll 'ave a drink, then,' Eddie Green said, 'and then we'll 'ave to find a taxi. . . .'

'It's only a couple of miles, chief. You can walk it. . . .'

Eddie Green stopped wiping his brow. He stood back and stared at the ticket-collector. 'Use a little bit of sense,' he said. 'My mate's not built for walking; see that, can't you? Swimming, yeah, but not walking. I take it you do 'ave taxis round 'ere?'

The ticket-collector stared at Kenny; but for the first time he could ever remember Kenny just held his head up and stared back. He didn't feel all embarrassed, as he usually did. The way Eddie Green had said it had made it sound quite all right to be the way he was.

'Over there,' the man said, and he turned away, back into his little room.

'Come on,' said Eddie Green. 'At least we can put some water on this fire.' He led the way across the road into a pub and pointed to some seats just inside the door. Kenny kept his eyes on the floor. It was the sort of situation he hated. At his age he'd have looked out of place in here even if there hadn't been something about him which was out of the ordinary. As it was, he felt like something out of a circus at first, waddling in amongst all those men and squeezing himself into a circular wooden armchair. He looked up and saw all the faces which had gone silent to stare at him. But, 'You just sit there, son, and tell me if you ain't 'appy,' Eddie Green said; and everyone's attention twisted back to beer and conversation.

Kenny wasn't asked what he wanted. He was brought a lemonade and a bag of crisps. With all the heat, and being with Eddie Green, he hadn't realized how hungry he was; but after quenching the first part of his thirst he swallowed the crisps in three goes and made a start on what Eddie Green slid across of his own.

'I'll get some more in a bit, and a few bars of nutty. Then

what we've gotta do quick is get down the 'arbour and see if that boat's there.' He raised his voice. 'An' if it is, there ain't 'alf gonna be some ructions, I can tell you. If she's there. Or if she ever was!' He banged his glass down and Kenny jumped. 'Well, what d'you reckon? You know 'er, don't you? Is it likely she'd 'ide 'erself on some boat like that?'

Kenny tried to turn down the corners of his mouth in a don't-know look, but it didn't really feel any different to a silly smile. The trouble was, he *knew* she was on it, didn't he? He'd seen her, on the deck with the others, waving. Up there in full view, she'd been, so she must have conned them into giving her a ride. Yeah, she'd definitely gone with it, he knew that. But telling that to Eddie Green—that was different. He'd gone too far already, by talking about the boat in the first place. So now he had to be not too sure at all.

'I dunno if she would. She's not silly—not to go off with no strangers. . . .'

Eddie Green thought for a moment. 'Yeah, you say that; but then would you 'ave said she'd run off any'ow? If you can do one stupid thing you can do another!'

It was hard for Kenny, putting a blank face on all those back-stairs conversations running through his mind; Patsy swearing about Eddie Green, and trying to cover up the red marks; but he tried looking dim, the way he acted for the kids.

Eddie Green looked at him through the glass he was holding up. 'Any'ow, you know 'er,' he said, 'so just tell me, Ken, why a girl like that, with all the opportunities I've given 'er—a nice 'ome of her own, an' a father, which she never 'ad before—tell me why she should suddenly do a bunk. She wasn't in no trouble, was she?'

Kenny shook his head. Not the way Eddie Green meant, not at school, she wasn't.

'So why? I ask you, why?'

It was always so hard when people got close to you like this, asked you confidential questions. It was like his mum sitting on the bed. Being like this clammed him up even when he had got something to say. Like now, for instance. All right, he knew why she'd gone, and he could have told the man: he could have told him, 'You're selfish and spiteful and shouldn't be allowed within a mile of Patsy!' But of course he'd never have the guts to say that, that was for sure. On the other hand, there was *something* he could tell the man, to make up a bit to Patsy for saying about the boat: something which would help him see why Patsy was doing what she was. But this close, confidential thing ... Kenny knew he couldn't say it this close.... He shrugged. 'Search me,' he said.

And that ended that. To Kenny's great relief, Eddie Green moved away and went to buy some more crisps and a bar of chocolate, and got the landlord to give him a plastic carrier-bag. They went out into the late afternoon heat and found a stifling taxi: and within ten minutes they were standing outside another pub, in Queenborough.

Just ahead of them, facing away from the pub, a long jetty ran out to where a narrow channel funnelled through a wide expanse of shallow mud. A few boats were leaning there, but Kenny quickly saw that they were all too small: there was nothing remotely like the long, wide boat he'd seen Patsy on in the creek. He looked across the water beyond at the burn-off flame above the oil refinery. God, this was hot and depressing! All he really wanted now was the shade of his bedroom at home.

'Well?' Eddie Green asked him, sharply.

'No!' he jumped, 'it ain't one of those. . . .'

'Bloody wild goose chase!' Eddie Green turned and stumped in through the open door of the pub. Inside, two men in yachting caps were smoking pipes and saying nothing, staring out through the entrance. Eddie Green walked up to the bar between their stools. He didn't wait for the landlord to appear. 'You 'aven't seen. . . .' he began; 'no, 'old on. . . .' He called Kenny in. 'Tell 'em about the boat,' he said. 'See if these blokes've seen anything like it.'

Kenny told them, keeping it as vague as he could, while the

landlord came from behind his curtain to lean on the bar and listen.

'Well, it's just a boat, only big, sort of, and blue down the sides; and white on the top bits. . . .'

But from the moment he opened his mouth the two men with pipes were shaking their heads.

'Only just got in on the tide.'

'Nothing like that when I berthed.'

'Hold on a minute, son. Why d'you want to know?' the landlord asked slowly, as if he were taking charge of things. 'What's your business?'

Eddie Green ran a look over him. 'Business of a missing person,' he said; 'my daughter, as it 'appens; young girl, about so 'igh, run off from Deptford. . . .'

'Deptford?' The landlord raised an eyebrow, and very deliberately pushed an evening paper round to Eddie Green.

He and Kenny stepped up; and with frowns on their faces they both read the stop-press. Kenny felt a sudden hunger inside, and his tongue went dry in the roof of his mouth. Even Eddie Green looked choked. Patsy sounded very important in that short couple of lines, Kenny thought, more like a TV star who's done a bunk on her family; and it seemed peculiar, made you tingle, reading about her all that way away on a pub bar down in Kent. Just like all the murdered kids you saw in the papers. . . .

'Yeah, that's 'er. An' I'm 'er father.'

'Well, I'm sorry, squire, I haven't seen her. But I have seen a biggish boat, blue and white, like the one the boy mentioned; she was here last night, a keel barge of some sort, from what I could see from here. We were busy, mind, so I didn't take a lot of notice. But there was a crowd of young people in, sounded as if they'd come off her. Put off to Steeple Stones, mid-day, I think. No girl of this description, though, not in here. . . .'

Eddie Green remained staring at the landlord for a moment or two, like a doubting policeman seeking something more.

Then he looked down at the paper. There were no more words.

'Here.' The landlord held a glass up to the brandy optic and slid it across to Eddie Green. 'Drink that, squire. Make you feel better. And here's a Coke for your boy. . . .'

Eddie Green drank his brandy, still silent, not even a word of contradiction about Kenny. Kenny downed his Coke.

'What's the best way to Steeple Stones, then, guv'nor?'

'Well, there won't be a train till six o'clock in the morning. But what you want to do is go up to the police station. If you reckon she's on that boat, they'll run you round to Steeple Stones within the hour. . . .'

'Yeah,' said Eddie Green. 'Thanks.'

'Not at all, squire. Hope you find her.'

'Yeah. So do I.' Eddie Green walked past Kenny out of the bar.

The sun was lower now; the day had suddenly lost its heat; and Kenny shivered at the prospect which lay ahead.

8

The *Dame Sybil* was a tip of stage clothing and untidy laughter. But Patsy felt lost in all the diverse high spirits around her. There was nothing organized about what was going on, no common activity or general talk to involve her, just a lot of cheerful people mending or pressing costumes and going over some of their lines. Even Jenny had forgotten her as she and Ruth rehearsed the opening to one of their scenes.

But it wasn't that. It was Patsy's own worries that were cutting her off like deafness: anxieties all wrapped up with the man at the other end of the long cabin who was sitting as quietly as she in all the turmoil, tinkering with a small spotlight. He kept looking up to take out his pipe and throw a joke in here, another friendly glance at Patsy through there. But if he fooled all of them, he didn't fool her.

Miss Bligh. That had done it. She hadn't cottoned when he'd said it at first; well, not properly; but the second time she had. *Green* was her name to all these people, Patsy Green, because of what had been on the note. But he'd called her Bligh, on purpose, twice, just to show her he knew. And that was why he was sitting there watching her worry over what he was going to do about it. He'd seen the paper somewhere, or found the torn piece—you didn't have to be brilliant to work that out. But he hadn't said anything, not yet; and that was the tricky bit; that was what was worrying her. . . .

Patsy blew out her cheeks and looked at the steps up to the wheel-house. Time to clear off, wasn't it? She struggled to visualize the map Jenny had shown her. Was she near enough to Margate to make it, if she went now? That red road on the map had looked very long: fifteen miles, or something, Jenny had said: no five minute trot, you could bet on that. Which probably meant she wouldn't get anywhere near Mrs Broadley before they grabbed her, not if she went too soon— because this lot would all be shooting straight to the nearest policeman, just to put themselves in the right over bringing her.

But then if she wasn't near enough to make it, how long had she got before Joe told everyone about her? Hell! The crying shame of it was, with the boat going all the way to Margate in the next couple of days, Joe was forcing her to dive out of her hiding-place before she'd made full use of it.

Stay, or make the move: that was the big problem. She felt like a lady on a tightrope, stuck in the middle with no going forward and no going back; having to stay there and put on a great big false smile, until she fell!

'And how about our little star of the future, how's she?' Jenny had turned back to her. 'Went well, lovey, didn't it? Weren't you pleased with yourself?'

'Yeah,' said Patsy. 'I s'pose so. It's tomorrow, though, that's what puts the wind up me: with all the people there.' Well, that was the sort of thing Jenny would expect her to say.

'Quite right, lovey, stay nervous. Once you get complacent, it goes; you lose the edge of your performance. Did you enjoy it, though, the way you thought you would?'

'Yeah. Not 'alf. Great. No, I really liked it....' Patsy tried to dredge up her original show of enthusiasm. Whatever was in Joe's mind, she'd better not forget the reasons why the others had brought her.

'Pity Mum and Dad can't see you, eh?'

'Yeah. But Jason ... they're up the hospital all the time....' The last thing she wanted was some well-meaning twit going back in the van to fetch them down to see her act!

'Never mind, lovey. Perhaps one day. Now look, we're all going to pop into town for a little drink, help us unwind. What would you like to do? You can come with us—we'll find some place with a little garden—or you can stay here. It's up to you.

Either way, it's only for an hour or so before the pubs close. . . .'

Patsy's reply was immediate. 'Stay here,' she said. 'I'm a bit tired. I'll be all right.' She kept her voice calm. Don't get too excited, she told herself. But this was a chance out of the blue! On her own she could look up that map again. And if she decided to go, she could do it without being stopped—*and* get an hour's start.

'All right, lovey. We won't be far away: just up the road at the Anchor. We'll bring you back a Coke and some crisps.'

'Oh, thanks.'

'And if you want to turn in, there's nothing to stop you. You've had quite a day.'

'Yeah. O.K.' She could say that again!

It was very quiet when they'd all gone. Just a clump of feet on the deck, and that was it. Joe she watched all the way. At first she was scared he might stay; but he didn't; he couldn't really; not with him being the man with the friends down here. He didn't look at her as he sidled past to the steps: just went out normally, with all the others. No one would have guessed.

On her own, Patsy sat up and listened. During the day she'd got so used to the slap and seethe of the shingle in the waves that she'd stopped hearing it. But now she heard it again: that, and the distant sound of a crowd of kids along the front; and a motor-bike doing a racing start away from somewhere. She had suddenly become very aware of everything around her. Inside the boat, though, it was unnaturally quiet. There were no more jokes, or cassettes, or snatches of lines from the play. It was all very lonely, really—and Patsy wasn't used to being alone. There was always Jason annoying, or her mother moaning, or Eddie Green bursting in to shout at her; and today there'd been these people laughing. But as she began to realize that she was in nobody's charge for the next hour, that there was nobody to tell her what to do, nobody to look after her—down in that boat, with only the one way out—all at once she began to feel really nervous. Her eyes darted this way and that; her ears twitched all around.

Oh, come off it, girl! She was the kid who'd run away, wasn't she? Wasn't this just what she'd wanted? she told herself. 'Course it was. Right! So now she had to be tough. She had to look up that map, and if she could work out a way to Margate she had to get some food and money and get off this boat while she could. She'd been found out, that was what she had to remember, not worry about the sound of the water.

Like a big hand the water moved beneath her, but Patsy did her best to ignore the creaking of the boat. Steeling herself, she climbed up behind Joe's bunk and pulled out a handful of glossy maps. The covers slid in her nervous fingers as she scanned the outline diagrams beneath the titles to find the one she wanted: 'Canterbury and East Kent: Sheet 179'. Got it! And there was Margate up in the top right hand corner, like 'home' in a game of Snakes and Ladders. Clumsily, she unfolded it on the bunk and ran her finger along that long thin road from Steeple Stones to Margate. Yeah, that was it, fifteen miles—a hell of a way: nearly the whole width of the map: definitely not a distance she could walk in an hour or so. She looked up at the ship's clock above the stairway. Quarter to nine. No, there was no way she could ever make Margate before the morning, even if she went this minute. Not walking. Anyway, she thought despondently, what chance would a kid like her stand, walking along that road in the night, with everyone looking out for her? No chance at all. The only other thing was a ride: but who'd give her a lift this time of night without reporting her to someone—or murdering her!

Well, that was no good. So what *was* she going to do? She started to re-fold the map.

Hold on! Wait a minute, what was that? What was that thin black line running along to Margate, straighter than the road? Bending her head low over the map Patsy made another journey with her finger. Well, it was obvious, wasn't it? It wasn't a road, or a river. It was the railway. You could see the little red dots for the stations: Steeple Stones, Herne Bay, somewhere in between, then Margate.

What about the railway, then? Patsy's heart was palpitating, and her eyes had widened. Now there was a sudden ray of hope. How about taking some money and catching a train? It wasn't all that late for trains, she could well remember them rattling on in the evenings from her old bedroom at Mrs Broadley's house. Then why not go on one of them?

She knew why not. She was too young. They wouldn't even let her through the gates without a load of questions—and they'd soon remember her going through when everyone started chasing. Morning time would be all right, going to school time; but not now, on a Saturday night; and especially not after what was in the paper. She'd be picked up quicker than a quid on the pavement, and it'd be home to Eddie Green and the thrashing of her life before midnight. No, she was definitely too young to go on the railway. If only she looked older. They wouldn't take no notice of her then, not down here at the seaside in the summer time.

Patsy jumped off Joe's bunk so fast she hit her head on the light fixing. Silly idiot, why hadn't she thought of that before? The make-up. She could look a hell of a lot older with make-up on: just do what Jenny had done for the play, and then do the eyes up a bit more, put more red on the lips. There were plenty of clothes around: stuff from the theatre: a pair of high heels, and she could roll up some tights in Ruth's other bra. She'd get by then, all right. She was tall enough. And she'd be all right if she got in a carriage with plenty of other people. Yeah! Do that and with any luck she be down in Margate with Mrs Broadley almost as quick as this lot getting back from the pub. After that Joe could go and tell who he liked!

Even as she was working things out, Patsy was frantically active. In no time she had Jenny's make-up bag on the table in the middle of the cabin, and a mirror propped up behind it. And with her hand as steady as she could keep it—what with her own excitement and the slight movement of the boat—Patsy started. First, her lips. She chose the orange-red Jenny had liked in the theatre—the one she'd blotted on the strip from the paper. But she found it wasn't any easier now than it had been when she'd done it as a little kid: she got it on her teeth and looked like Dracula till she'd rubbed it off. Then it went where it shouldn't round her mouth, and she looked like a clown. And all the time the *Dame Sybil* creaked eerily, and the water moved her. But after a lot of swearing and two false starts she had it more or less right—quite good enough for the screaming rush she was in, anyhow. Now her eyes, and that'd be that. Carefully, but shaking more than ever round this delicate zone, Patsy outlined them in black, just as Jenny had done, and filled in the lids with the handiest blue in the bag.

Come on! They'd still be sitting back in the pub now; but time was going fast. She grabbed the mirror and looked in it. Oh, yes, she'd put on five years, easy. Now, some padding in the bra, a sparkly shawl off Ruth's bunk, Jenny's shoes, and then it was find a quid somewhere, and away! She smiled tensely at the reflection of herself. No, her hair. Better do something about her hair. That looked a right load of tat! Quickly, kicking off her plastic sandals, finding a wide hair band, grabbing then discarding the bra, Patsy finished off. Now, that quid. . . .

The *Dame Sybil* gave a lurch. And a bump. What was that? Patsy turned to ice. Was it a bigger wave? Or another boat bashing her? There was a clump overhead. Footsteps! There was someone up there on the deck. . . .

She whirled about feverishly, didn't know what to do. Hide! It could be anyone up there: someone she knew, someone who'd found her out, or someone who'd seen the lights, looked at her through the portholes—some barmy, like that man in the creek. Hide, then! Hide! Get in the lav.

But the shawl was tangled in Jennie's bunk drawer, and she had to rip . . . RIP . . . it out. Quick! The lav! That was the only hiding place there in the main cabin. But it was beyond and beneath the wheel-house steps: and already one foot, two feet, were coming slowly down through the wheel-house opening on to the treads.

At that moment Patsy was petrified beyond screaming. She just stood in her finery and watched him come with an awful fascination.

The corduroy trousers gave him away. It was Joe. And now Patsy realized that since the first footstep on the deck she'd known that that was who it would be. She didn't move. She stood with her back to the table, like some heroine in a silent movie.

'Hello, sweetheart, it's only me. Guess who was stupid and left his tobacco behind?'

He came down into the cabin and stood at the foot of the steps. He made no move to look for any tobacco.

'And what's Patsy doing with herself while everybody's out?' He'd noticed the make-up, but he was smiling at her genially, like the Joe she'd had a laugh with the night before.

'I been ... er ... dressing up ... pretending ... you know....'

'Yes, I know. I should think you've had to get pretty good at that, sweetheart. Pretending. Eh?' He walked over towards her, patting his trouser pockets for his pipe. 'Been making-up, too, have you?' He was staring her in the face.

Patsy nodded. She was aware of every line, every hair, every pore on his face: and yet she could see nothing but his unblinking grey eyes.

'I was trying to make myself look like Ruth. You know ... glamorous ....' she tailed off, not even convincing herself.

'Oh, I see.' Joe sat down on a chair between the table and his bunk and crossed his legs. He slid a tobacco tin out of the drawer and started to fill his pipe. 'And you're wearing that orange lipstick, eh?'

Patsy tried to move her lips, but they seemed to have let her down. She still couldn't move, couldn't even contemplate a dash for the steps. *That orange lipstick.* Just as she'd thought, he'd found the screwed-up paper in that box of lights.

'Well, now, I want you to listen to me for a minute, Patsy.' He got his pipe going in thick, successful, puffs. 'Listen to me for a bit. . . .'

Patsy swallowed. What was he going to say? Would it be what she was frightened of?

'. . . It's Patsy Bligh, isn't it? The young lass who's run away from home? Isn't that right?'

Patsy's mouth opened and closed in a yes.

'Well, why don't you tell me all about it, sweetheart? We've got plenty of time before the others get back.'

Patsy stared at his lips as they mouthed the words, as they clenched the pipe round his teeth. Why was that? *Before the others get back*. Did that mean he wasn't going to say anything to the others tonight? Was he trying to tell her he was going to keep her secret, then? As usual, when she was uncertain, she started to say something.

'Well . . . I was just . . . fed up with it at home,' she said. 'I was always . . . you know . . . getting into trouble. And he kept hitting me.'

'Oh, what for? Didn't you see eye to eye?'

'No, not specially.' She shut her mouth, tight. He wasn't going to know about all that other business, whatever else she had to say to play him along and keep him occupied. . . .

'Well, have you considered that perhaps he had reason, sweetheart? It was very naughty of you to play that trick with the letter, wasn't it? For instance, can you imagine what trouble I can get into, as skipper, for agreeing to bring you along?' He knocked some spit out of his pipe. 'And Pete? What about him? He's going to look silly, isn't he?'

'Yeah. I s'pose so. . . .'

'But now, you see, the big trouble is, I know—don't I, Patsy?' He tried to look reasonable, matter-of-fact. 'The others probably won't guess—they won't see any papers, and the Steeple Stones people will naturally think you're really with us, no need for them to suspect a thing. . . . But I *know*, that's the trouble. And where do you think that leaves me when you're caught? If I don't turn you in straight away I could very probably go to prison. . . .'

Patsy could only stare at him. Was that so? Well, that was it, then. This was the end of the road for her. He'd have to tell someone; unless for some reason he was trying to work out something else. . . .

'Now, look, I'm going to put this to you. Because I'm a great friend of Pete's and seeing how well you're doing for him in your little scene . . . and because I'm very fond of you . . . like an uncle. . . .' He was looking at her very straight. 'If I don't say anything to anyone now, when the time comes—and it must Patsy, we both know that—will you make me a solemn promise you won't ever let on that I knew?

'Let me find out when the others do, eh? . . . and meanwhile give yourself a few more days with us, and a bit of a chance to do the play. . . .'

Wait a minute. What was this? Was he trying to do some sort of a deal? Like a faulty engine picking up, Patsy found she was starting to breathe easier again. 'Yeah,' she said. 'If you like. . . .'

'All right then. It's a deal.' Just like that, all over and done with. 'And don't let anyone ever say I wasn't all for a spirit of adventure.'

Another sudden bump—and a crash this time: the sound of feet landing on the deck.

'Hey, down there! Come on, Joe! We're going on to Lornie's house, and they all reckon you don't know where it is.' It was Bob, poking his head down through the hatch like a crazy marionette.

'Yes, O.K.,' said Joe, huffing and puffing busily with his pipe and his tobacco tin. 'You're quite right, I don't, Bob.'

'You coming, girlie?' Bob asked. 'We might be back late. . . .'

'Yeah, I'm coming!' Patsy said. 'Just wash my face. . . .'

Bob frowned at her made-up face. 'Yeah, I should think so, too. Come on, then, hurry up.'

Patsy ran to the small basin in the galley and rubbed cruelly at her cheeks with a cloth. You bet she was going with them, she told the cold water. Sitting all done-up in a train didn't appeal to her any more, no more than waiting here did–not if there was a remote chance she could still get what she wanted. Not while it looked as if she was being given that chance. . . .

9

The flicker of the fire seemed to draw the world in around them; and for once Kenny didn't feel threatened by the feeling of closeness. Perhaps it was because they were out of doors, or perhaps because there was a dividing film of dark between them, as if they were immersed in water. Or perhaps it was because of what had recently happened. Kenny didn't know. But he still felt excited, he was very aware of that. Getting a bus back over the bridge off the Isle of Sheppey had been a long and boring business, but in a way even doing it had been a surprise; and then it had led to this.

'Forget the police,' Eddie Green had said. 'We'll keep them out o' this unless we 'ave to. . . .' and he'd headed them back towards the road to Steeple Stones. 'We'll get as far as we can tonight, an' then we'll kip down in some pub: make an early start in the morning. . . .'

Kenny hadn't thought about spending the night away from home. He never had thought about it, because it wasn't something he'd ever done: there weren't any aunts or uncles who'd have him, nor cousins who couldn't wait for him to go and stay: so the prospect of a strange bed didn't conjure any experiences to feed his thoughts; and he'd just tagged along, a shuffle behind Eddie Green, and thought those other thoughts instead about Patsy in the paper, and how Eddie Green was playing into both their hands by not going to the police. One more night, then, he'd thought; all the more time for her to put herself out of his reach.

But what had happened next had sent all that skimming— discarded thoughts like flat stones on the water—and he and Eddie Green had ended up like this: together. Probably, getting into trouble with someone else did make you more matey with them, Kenny thought; it could be that was one of the things he missed out on by being so much on his own at school. Anyway, he'd certainly had a taste of being in something together when he'd stood with Eddie Green in that pub doorway close to closing and the bloke had said No Way! He'd looked at them with his suspicious little eyes, the man and the fat kid, travelling together, wanting a room late in the evening.... Yeah, his eyes had said it all. Distrust. The look of something wrong. 'No, mate, we don't 'ave no accommodation. Not round here. Perhaps down the seaside....' And that time the stares in the bar had persisted; and like a real physical pressure they'd served to close the door on Kenny and Eddie Green.

And that had been that. Eddie Green had sworn his head off, cursing in amongst it all for not bringing the paper with him; and they'd walked away in a muttering mood of bitter rejection towards the next cluster of buildings, in the hope that it contained another pub they might try. But it hadn't; and in spite of himself Kenny had lagged behind so that in the end their sense of defeat had been spiritual, physical, and in a strange way, mutual.

Finally, in what had seemed to be the last of the light, Eddie Green had said it. 'All right. In these trees 'ere. I know what we'll bloody do....'

Now, after the long and tiring day on trains and buses and on foot, Kenny had been given a new lease of life helping Eddie Green to make the camp, like being in a war film, or Robin Hood. The man had disappeared for half an hour while Kenny stooped to gather wood in the dusk, and had come back with string and a big plastic sheet, quickly rigging up a bivouac between two bushes. Then he'd set about building a fire, showing Kenny how to cut out the turf with a knife and hollow out one end to create an updraught: Eddie Green had got a new lease of life, too, it seemed: and when the fire was crackling well, out of his shirt had come the earthy potatoes.

'Come on,' he'd said, 'we'll 'ave these taters in their

overcoats,' and he'd pricked them and buried them deep in the hot glow, and prodded them about with a stick till they were evenly black all over. Kenny had sat, cross-legged and fascinated, till finally, wrapping leaves round them, Eddie Green had knocked off the worst of the cracking black and thrown a couple over for Kenny to pass the hot bites about in his mouth.

'Lovely, them. We'll leave a few in the embers for the morning: now we'll just 'ave the best of this fire and go off for a kip when it's quiet. . . .' Eddie Green had settled over the fire, crouching like a picture of a caveman, relaxed in an alert sort of way, and they'd talked: and for the first time in a long while Kenny didn't feel threatened at all.

'Better this way. We ain't beholden to no one, like this. If she ain't on that boat the police'll start looking at us like a couple of idiots, like, as if we're wasting their time, or putting 'em off the trail. . . . But this way, see, we'll still be there early, soon as the buses start running. 'Long as you don't mind sleeping rough one night. . . .'

Kenny shook his head. 'No.' Mind? Of course he didn't mind. It'd be a change from his old lady coming in and sitting on the bedclothes.

'I been in that phone by the bus stop. Rang your mum. Patsy still ain't there. . . .'

'Oh.' Of course, Patsy! For half an hour Kenny had forgotten what all the drama was about. Still free, then, was she? That meant she was doing all right: a second night out. She could even have made it by now.

'An' they know we won't be 'ome tonight. Mind you, they think we're in some pub somewhere, sleeping.' Eddie Green grunted. 'Waste of money that, I reckon, when you know 'ow to live off the land. Eh?'

'Yeah.' And you were private, too, you didn't have to keep meeting people, Kenny thought. No, it was definitely all right, this, being your own boss. He could picture himself at it: and that was something rare.

Eddie Green lit a cigarette with an ember, and the two of them hunched there with the plastic at their backs. The wood crackled, and from the distant A2 the drone of vehicles drifted over the trees. Kenny squinted at the man through the smart of wood-smoke. He looked as much at home crouching there as he had sitting in his armchair in the flats.

'Did they learn you how to do this in the army?' he asked. 'Camping out?'

Eddie Green's attention came back from a long way away. 'No, son! No chance of that. I wouldn't entertain the army! I taught myself living rough. Doing it, and reading about it. . . .'

'Oh.'

'Not books, though.' He said it as if that would have been unthinkable. 'Papers.'

Kenny could see his eyes glowing in the firelight. The man fell silent for a moment, but Kenny knew he'd go on.

'See, when I was a kid we was all full of this crook, killer, shot two coppers and got away, disappeared off the face of the earth. It was all over the papers for weeks and weeks, on account of they couldn't find 'im anywhere. Everyone was scared, wondering where 'e'd turn up—would 'e walk through their back door one dark night? There was this great big search—but no sign. Anyway, it turned out what 'e'd done was, 'e'd found this thick wood, and lived in it all this time in a bivouac, a bit like this, but all camouflaged up. People searching walked past within yards and never see it. Only 'e got careless in the end, and one night the smoke from 'is fire got seen. . . .

'Well, I read all about that, an' I took it all in, like you do: and then once when I fell out with my old man, I done it myself. Only for a week-end, like. But look as 'ard as they could, they couldn't find me nowhere. I got fed up in the end and come out—and did I get a belting off my old man when I walked in 'ome!' Eddie Green laughed thinly, kicking the dying fire with his boot. 'Yeah,' he said, serious again. 'But I showed 'em.'

'Yeah.' Kenny felt uncertain about saying too much. When people got a bit confidential you either shut up or you changed the subject. At least, that's what he had to do with his mum.

'Yeah, I was all choked to begin with, the way you are after a bust up, then I got into it and I really 'ad a good time making that camp. I was my own boss, see, and no one knew where I was. Getting free for a bit, that was it. It does you good. Did it a lot after that, an' all, till the old man snuffed it.' Eddie Green poked a new log he'd just thrown on, and it suddenly burst into a rotten flame. He stared at it. 'Yeah. Funny, forgot all this, I 'ad, till today. And the swimming, an' the green towers. God, it don't 'alf take you back. . . .'

Kenny let him stare into the smoky fire in peace, remembering things. The man threw on yet another piece of wood, as if he didn't want to let the fire die down.

'Where'd you get the spuds?' Kenny suddenly asked.

'Oh, some bloke's allotment up the road. They ain't very deep, an' a pair of 'ands is good enough in well-turned earth. 'E won't miss the couple we've 'ad, will 'e?'

'No.' Kenny felt quite conspiratorial, sitting there. It was good, round a fire—except your front got very hot and your back felt cold, sort of dividing you down the middle. But why worry? It was a lot better than sitting round the telly in that poky little room at home.

Eddie Green didn't seem to want to be drawn into talking about the potatoes, though. He was really feeding the fire now, with snappy twigs and crumbling pieces of mossy branch, creating smoke and noise and warmth. 'Yeah, it's interesting,' he was saying, his eyes in the flames, 'what comes back to you after all those years. . . .'

'I was gonna say,' said Kenny, sensing the mood of the past and feeling easy in himself, 'what was those big green things?'

The man stopped with a piece of wood poised in his hand. He squinted across at Kenny, and he didn't move for a good five seconds. Then into the flames it went. 'Well, I dunno what they was for,' he said, 'something to do with storing stuff for loading on to ships. Starch, or something. But they was 'igh, I can tell you that, an' what I used to do was I climbed up 'em, up a ladder on the inside, and got out on the top, and then I jumped across 'em, from one to the other, like. When I felt bad. . . .'

Kenny frowned. He didn't understand that.

'It was like this—an' you might cotton or you might not, but this is 'ow it went—' Eddie Green leant forward with his hands dangling across his knees. 'My old man and me, we didn't 'it it off, right? Weren't the best of friends. I was a bit on the small side, an' 'e was a great mountain of a man.' Eddie Green snorted. 'No one ever 'ad an argument with my old man on 'is own. So I didn't come off too strong, you know what I mean? The old lady stuck up for me now and again, but there's no two ways about it, to 'im I was bad news. An' like it 'appens, the more I tried, the worse I got. . . .'

His eyes were half closed, and now he could have been telling all this to Kenny, or just explaining some memory to himself.

'. . . We're digging the garden an' I can't keep my end up, I get one row done to 'is ten. So 'e ain't pleased. 'E gets me painting the ceiling while 'e's doing a door, and I can't keep going fast enough to keep the edge alive. It ends up all blotchy. Again, 'e ain't pleased. The van won't start an' I'm no good for pushing, an' my feet don't reach the pedals for letting in the clutch. All that sort of thing.' His voice went very low. 'Some days I 'ated 'is guts so much I was planning 'ow I was gonna kill 'im in the night. I'm praying to God for the strength. But I know 'e'd wake up an' 'ave me. So I got used to letting it out other ways. . . .'

Kenny sat with his head back and tried to keep an expressionless look on his face.

'. . . Yeah, after one of those do's I'd clear off on my bike an' do stupid things— like deliberately go swimming when the water was dangerous, or go chasing across the railway line so close to a train I can't risk a slip—or I go up the towers an' jump till I feel better.' He tapped Kenny on the knee as if he thought he wasn't listening. 'See, the way them towers was built, a little kid could jump across near the middle, where they nearly touched: the jump next to the gangway's only about two feet across. But as you go further sideways so your jump 'as to get bigger an' bigger to get you over. Some days when I was in a real state I'd jump along the three of 'em, hell or nothing, as wide, or wider, as I reckon I can push myself, where it's over on to the next one or down fifty feet to the ground. An' I've proved something, see? So I feel a bit better, just being alive, I s'pose, an' off on my bike before the foreman catches me. . . .'

Kenny measured the towers inside his head—Eddie Green would definitely have killed himself if he'd missed his jump.

'. . . See, I'm so bloody miserable I'm either gonna kill myself doing it, or prove to myself it don't matter a toss what my old man thinks of me, because I've got guts. . . .'

Kenny's chins concertina'd in a slow nod. Eddie Green wasn't on his own. He could think of more than one who felt like that. . . .

He said nothing. For a moment the only sound was the fire snapping and thudding, while the smoke rose up between the trees in white signals.

'. . . So that's the story of the towers.'

'Yeah.' Be matter-of-fact, that was the best way, Kenny decided. And don't push your luck by asking any more questions. . . .

With a big sigh Eddie Green suddenly stood up. The confidential moment was over. ''Ere we'd better let this die down. Don't want the Old Bill thinking we're tramps or poachers. We'll see this safe, then I've found a stack for a warm kip. . . .'

'What, you mean a hay stack?'

'Yeah, a little one, what's left of it. Just down the road a bit. . . .'

'Oh.' Really surprising, Eddie Green was turning out to be, Kenny thought.

'Well, when you're fit. I mean, you didn't wanna go 'ome, did you?'

'No!' And Kenny meant it. Who'd have thought it? For once in his life he was really enjoying himself.

The haystack was small: just a few bales left from the winter feeding in an untidy corner of a field, jumped down low— probably by local kids who played safer games than Eddie Green ever had. It was nearly dark now, the sky just holding out in deep blue before the black. Unselfconsciously, the man relieved himself into the hedge. So did Kenny. It seemed to make a lot of noise in spite of his care, and he strained his ears for footsteps. But it was very quiet now, just a few concrete houses as silent as pill boxes further down the road on the other side. Nobody about.

' 'Ere y'are. Worm yourself down under the 'ay. Pull plenty up an' round you....' Eddie Green helped Kenny to get himself buried. 'Get your feet in deep. It's cold feet what keep you awake. Now make a sort of pillow for your 'ead....'

Kenny made himself comfortable, building up here and shallowing out there, feeling the crackling hay give to the weight of his shape. Eddie Green did the same next to him. This'd be all right, Kenny thought: it was warm enough, you could shift about, and even though Eddie Green was close, the short stalks of bedding made it impossible to feel pressed down, like with bedclothes.

'Right, we won't do no more talkin', then. We'll get straight off. The sun'll 'ave us up early tomorrow....'

'Yeah, O.K.'

Still the cars droned on the distant A2, but between the two of them there was a very long silence, with Kenny's eyes wide open to the sky. He looked around the huge horizon, and wondered at the vast pattern of points above him. God, the world was big. He saw the sudden movement of a shooting star etch itself half-way down across the heavens.

112

''Night,' said Eddie Green.

''Night,' said Kenny. But it was a long time before he wanted to close his eyes. Staring up at the immensity of the universe made him feel very, very small: and tonight that, too, brought him a strange sort of comfort.

It seemed only five minutes later when a chill new light opened his eyes again. The stars had gone, as if they'd been nothing but a dream, and so had Eddie Green. Kenny looked around for him, but he wasn't anywhere in sight. Kenny wasn't worried, though. He was getting used to the man's ways. He knew he'd be back in a while with the potatoes from the embers, and then they'd be off. So Kenny lay there and listened to the bright cheeping of the birds; and being so still he saw one of them, a minute and insistent creature sitting lightly on a leaf stem. A wren, he thought. And making that terrific noise!

It was comfortable, lying there like that, luxurious; but he'd better show a bit of willing, he decided—before Eddie Green came back. Like a waking corpse he sat up, scattering hay on either side: and he went to the bushes again, but noisier this time, and more confident than the night before.

'Come on, then!' The small head hardly reached to the top of the hedge. 'I've give you 'alf 'our extra. Got a bit of breakfast. Come on!'

Oh, no! Eddie Green sounded ratty again, as if he hadn't been to sleep at all. Miserable. Perhaps the man thought he'd said too much the night before. . . .

Kenny moved as quickly as he could. The wiry man led the way up the road at a good pace, and Kenny had to break into an awkward run to keep up. When they got to the fire in the small clearing he found out why. Wood smoke hung in the wet trees like filmy tights in the bathroom: but the smell was that of a cooked breakfast in the kitchen: and sure enough, there it was, frying bacon. Two rashers curling in their own fat on a foil tray.

'Got it off the milkman,' Eddie Green explained in a flat

voice. 'Milkmen come in 'andy, early in the morning. . . .'

Kenny's mouth was already watering, and he watched fascinated as the man hooked up a rasher with a firm twig and put it between two pieces of bread from a cut loaf on the ground.

' 'Ere y'are.'

'Ta.' Kenny took the bacon sandwich and stood eating it while Eddie Green handed him a small carton of cold milk.

'All right?'

'Yeah! All right.' Kenny nodded as he chewed. Well, it had been all right last night, and it'd probably get better again today. He hoped so, because somehow, with Eddie Green last night, even the breathless business of getting about hadn't seemed as bad as it usually did. Out here like this, with country instead of walls, being fat had been pushed to the back of Kenny's mind, like when he was in the water. And that had been a new treat. But he could tell that there was something up this morning. Things were different again, as if Eddie Green was trying to cover up the glimpses of that other person Kenny had seen. The boy burped at the milk and smiled with a white moustache at Eddie Green. 'This is tasty, this. . . .'

'Now we'll just finish it and kick the fire in, and we'll get up on the main road. . . .'

Kenny nodded.

'. . . An' we'll get off. Only thing is, I don't know which way to go. . . .' The man frowned at Kenny, definitely the old Eddie Green. Kenny frowned back. 'Well,' the man grumbled, 'I'm thinking she probably weren't on that bloody boat at all. If she's anywhere she's like as not still up Deptford—the little madam. . . .' He started chewing on his own bacon sandwich like a mean kid with his playground lunch, fast, and ready to move off quickly.

Drained by a sudden sense of disappointment, Kenny stood back on his heels. Oh, no! he thought. Go home now? After all this? What day was it, Sunday? Go home now and be back by dinner time, and have the usual Sunday sitting in that hot room with his mother all over him? Watching rubbish on the box till his old man came in from fishing? No thank you, not if he could help it: not when he'd been starting to enjoy these things they were doing: not when there was a chance it might last for another day or so. . . .

'Oh, no, she was definitely on it.' He'd said it before he knew it, putting as much reassurance into his voice as he could.

'Eh?' Eddie Green had stopped chewing and was looking at Kenny with eyes that were never going to blink.

'Well, I'm dead sure I did see her, or someone—you know, like her double. . . .'

'You talking about on the boat?'

'Yeah. I definitely reckon it was her. . . .'

'Do you? But you never said *definitely* before.'

'No. Well, I was pretty sure, but I didn't want to . . . you know . . . make no one think it was definite in case . . . you know . . . in case, well, it *was* just someone like her. But in my own mind I definitely reckon. . . .'

'That it was.'

Kenny's chins moved in a slow, serious nod.

'What was she wearing?'

'Her dress: the pink. . . .'

'Her cardigan. Did she 'ave 'er cardigan on?'

'No, I don't think so. . . .'

'No? Right, then it was 'er. It was 'er.' Eddie Green swigged back his milk like whisky. 'Yeah, well that's it. We'll get down Steeple Stones an' sort 'er out.' He spat out his bacon sandwich on to the fire, kicking the loose earth into the flames and killing the blaze kick by kick. 'Come on, then.' He suddenly cheered up again. 'Let's get off.'

But having said what he had, Kenny found he couldn't recover himself so quickly. He should have felt pleased, going to do what he wanted. But instead he felt more like a traitor now, selling Patsy short like that to buy himself more time.

He pushed out of the wood and puffed behind Eddie Green as the man led the way up the lane towards the coast road. What a let-down, feeling all mixed-up again.

Patsy had never really known a sleepless night before. Whatever had been on her mind, another row from Eddie Green, or trying not to sleep so she shouldn't wet the bed, she'd always gone off eventually: the same as she always had as a little kid, when she'd tried to stay awake for Father Christmas. But this Saturday night was different. The business with Joe had happened; being found out; and whatever he'd said it had thrown her completely.

After they'd got back from Lornie's and stumbled about, the men at their end of the cabin and the women at theirs, Patsy had sweated there on her bunk for hour after hour, her eyes roving over the low ceiling with its rusted points of condensation, while her active mind remembered everything that had happened to her. It was as if some robot in her brain knew she'd got herself in really deep now, and wasn't going to stop working until a solution had been found. The trouble was, it didn't seem to be finding any hopeful way out: there seemed to be no way round the fact that she didn't want an ally in Joe: her plans would have worked better without him. Now everything was going to be doubly difficult. Joe would be watching her; he'd be trying to protect her from herself. And she didn't want that. So she'd just tossed and turned and stewed until at last a dull flat light had reflected in off the water, and the dawn had come up from somewhere over Margate.

Hang on, that was all she could really do, she told herself. Keep a careful eye on Joe: stay in with him, but stay a distance away from him: and be ready to make a quick run for it when the time seemed right: before he could interfere. But that wasn't much to come up with for no proper sleep all night: and now, as the warmth of the sun seeped into the boat like a drowsy gas, she felt readier to sleep than she had for hours.

But there was no chance of a lie-in. Another run-through had been called, for the backstage people this time, and then Pete wanted to rehearse a couple of scenes again; so, Sunday or not, it wasn't going to be a day for lazing about. Patsy let everyone go to the small wash-space before she did: but her time came, and reluctantly she had to get up.

'Come on, lovey, chop-chop. This is the day, as they say. And there's tons to do before tonight. Then it's the big performance, and a party after. Oh, it's a hard life on the wicked stage!'

And that was no word of a lie, either, Patsy discovered. By the end of a hard morning's work she could see the amount of detailed effort that went into the simplest effect. All the timing that was necessary for a pistol to go off, or for the sound of a car drawing up to be right. And watching it, part of Patsy desperately wanted to care about how it all worked, to feel that she belonged enough to use their special theatre language. But she couldn't relax enough to enter into it: and she knew she wouldn't be around long enough to feel natural with it. And besides that, there was Joe. All she did, everywhere she went in the building, everything she said, happened with an acute awareness of Joe, the nag of wondering whether he was listening to her, looking at her, anticipating her next move. In the end she wasn't any of the Patsy's she could have been, she knew that. She wasn't the Patsy who would help Mrs Broadley and be a good granddaughter to her: she wasn't Eddie Green's bed-wetting little tyke: she wasn't Jenny's new friend, the lovable little cockney girl: and she wasn't the best new actress since Dame Sybil What's-her-name. She was a bit of each by turn, just a spoken sentence or a random thought at a time: but she was none of them for long, and she was thoroughly confused and unhappy.

But she worked hard. She fetched props and carried mugs, because she couldn't bear to sit and stew, and she did her scene again, walked it through and got the positions better, and then she did it all once more for the sake of the man on the lights. She was very tired by now, though, and she began to think she knew what it felt like to be drunk—with that strange awareness she'd had before of lots of things happening on different levels. There was what she was actually doing with her body; the knowing where Joe was and what he was up to; and beneath it all, deep inside, the very strong knowledge that she'd run away from home. And it wasn't till after their sandwiches on that second day, sitting in a corner of the converted church hall, that that bottom layer surfaced, and the true enormity of what she was doing rose up and hit her.

Suddenly it all seemed crazy. Patsy stared round at all these strangers' faces and began to feel really scared about what she'd done. *She'd run off from home*—and everybody back in Deptford would know about it by now. It would all be out in the open, like someone having a baby, or being in an accident; it was the sort of thing people didn't forget. 'She's the girl who ran away from home!' God! It was one thing to dream about it. Now she shivered at the unbelievable thought of what she'd actually done.

Eddie Green would kill her when he found her.

Yeah! *When* he found her. That was what she was really expecting, then. Not *if*. Her stomach tightened into a hard, tense muscle of fear. Of course she'd get caught. The roads between here and Mrs Broadley's were all open, not like the crowded little streets at home. Stupid, she'd been, to think she could get all the way down there without being picked up. Real stupid. It was only this crazy world of play-acting that had kept her fooling herself for so long. How daft could you get? Here she'd been, thinking she was getting away with it, and she was right in the muck, really.

'Getting nervous, Patsy? Come on, there's no need for that. . . .' Joe had walked round the table and was standing behind her, wrapping her in the comforting smell of his tobacco.

She shrugged her shoulders. 'No. Not really.' His big hand was on her arm, squeezing encouragement.

'That's my girl. That's my girl.'

She picked at some crisps. She closed her eyes and wanted to heave the biggest sigh of disappointment in the world. She didn't need this close attention. It hadn't been like this in her mind. She was being trapped in a net of sympathy. Which meant that getting caught and being sent back wouldn't take much at all—someone coming in with a newspaper, or a policeman turning up at the door. She'd give up, then, Eddie Green or no Eddie Green. She knew that. There wouldn't be any fight.

She was at a low ebb, and just then Mrs Broadley in Margate could have been on the other side of the world.

No, girl, she told herself, if she wasn't careful there wouldn't be much fight left in her at all....

10

He wasn't so bad, old Eddie Green, thought Kenny; a confirmation which helped him feel a bit better about what he'd said regarding Patsy being on the boat. The man had shown him all that outdoor survival stuff; and then on the bus to Steeple Stones he'd really put himself out to keep Kenny from feeling bad about being so big. He'd sat him in by the window on a double seat and taken the outside himself, with one foot out in the aisle. He'd made it look all natural and comfortable, even though it wasn't.

Eddie Green had organized it so that they took what breeze there was from an open window full in their faces, and Kenny was grateful for that, but as they got off the bus the morning heat hit them. It was frying weather; and by now everyone else was trailing about, getting more used to moving between drinks than between places. Already lemonade was scarce: and with no pubs open yet, Eddie Green ushered Kenny into the first cool confectioner's, where between them they burped their way through a bottle of cream soda.

'Right—manners—now we'll 'ave a good look along the front for this boat....'

Two ages met at Steeple Stones. Behind them a line of fisherman's cottages clung together, held up by the efforts of their London owners; and in front of them a reach of small boats was drawn up on the shelving beach; but it took no more than a quick look to see that these were little local boats, much too small to be the boat Kenny had seen Patsy on.

All the same, Eddie Green wanted to check them off with some sort of method. He led Kenny slowly along the line, asking him questions as they went.

'No, did you say?'

'Yeah. It's definitely not this one.'

'Why's that? Too big, too small, wrong colour? What?'

'Too small. It was bigger than that.'

' 'Ow bigger? Wider, longer, both?'

'Both.'

'Right.' Eddie Green nodded and they moved on to the next one.

'Same again. Too small all round.'

'Colour?'

'All wrong. This one's yellow.'

'And the other one was ... ?'

'Well, it was more ... white ... and blue....'

'Right. It's bigger all round, longer, wider, and it's white and blue. That's what we're after. Right?'

'Yeah, that's right.' He was being clever, Eddie Green, thought Kenny. He wasn't going to let him get away with being a bit hazy about it. He was making it so that *he* could spot the boat, with or without help, if he had to.

They got to the next one, but before Kenny could speak, Eddie Green had ruled it out for him. 'Too small by a long chalk, and wrong colours, right?'

'Yeah, that's right.'

Some of the boat owners were looking at them now; no doubt wondering what was going on, Kenny thought; and it stuck out a mile these Steeple Stones people weren't over the moon about being stared at by this hard, little bloke. They probably thought Eddie Green and him were sorting out a good boat to pinch, or break into. One man just stood and folded his arms, to let them know he was watching them.

But Eddie Green took no notice; he still moved on slowly, boat by boat, towards the harbour. ' 'Ow about this? Anything near the mark? It's bigger, i'n' it? An' it's blue an' white, like you said....'

Kenny looked at it critically. No. It was still too small. The deck on Patsy's boat had been wider, flatter, with more room

121

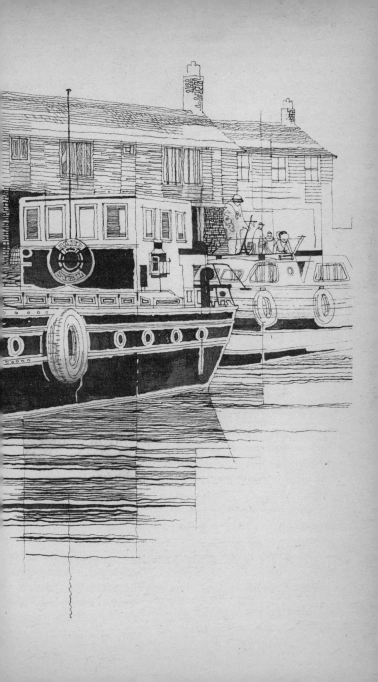

to move about on than this one had. 'No,' he said. But it was getting nearer the mark, and Kenny started to worry again about what he'd say to Eddie Green if they did come across the boat. That wasn't going to be one little bit easy: and it was getting more likely all the time. Well, he was just going to have to lie, wasn't he? There was no chance he'd give Patsy away, if he could help it. She was his friend. She'd never forgive him if she got caught.

But now the thought of being caught himself—caught between Patsy and Eddie Green—made Kenny's inside turn over. And what made it worse was it was more complicated than just the fear of crossing either of them. There was another bit to it. While there was no way he'd ever let Patsy down, now he had the funny feeling that he didn't want to let the man down, either. That was a stroke, he thought. From starting out hating him, now he was going to feel rotten about tricking Eddie Green.

Really, though, the plain fact of the matter was, there wouldn't be any option, would there? If they did see the boat, he couldn't say, 'Yeah, that's the one.' He'd have to try to put him off somehow. Especially after being selfish and stupid enough to tell his mum there actually had been a boat in the first place. All he could do was keep praying that the thing wasn't there, that the bloke in the pub at Queenborough had got it wrong. Then he could relax and enjoy what he'd pressed them on for, the day out with Eddie Green.

He tried to sit on a small wall, just to get his breath, but Eddie Green wasn't for resting yet: not with the harbour in sight.

'Come on,' he said, 'we're gonna check down there. If she's as big as you reckon, that's where she'll be, pound to a penny.'

And that's where she was. There was definitely no mistaking her when Kenny saw her again. Dazzling white in the sun, with her deep blue sides sliding down into the cool water, she looked every bit as special as Kenny had remembered.

Oh no! This was just what he'd dreaded. Kenny's spirits sank again. So he'd done it, hadn't he? Really clever, he'd been! He'd brought Eddie Green right to where she was: all for the easy way out; all by saying something he shouldn't, to stop his mum from pinning him down in his room; and then by saying something else to keep the jaunt with Eddie Green going. He'd actually led the hunt himself, right here to Patsy. What was it called? The *Dame Sybil*. Yeah, there was no doubt about it. This was the one. He could just see Patsy standing up at the front, waving at the man on the bank as if all her troubles were over for ever.

'So. The end of the line, eh, Ken?'

'What?'

' "What?" Come on, don't go telling me that ain't 'er. Blue sides, white deck, big, all clean and new-looking?'

Kenny frowned. 'No,' he said. He couldn't keep the desperation out of it. 'I dunno. No. It's *too* big. Them others was small, but I think this one's too big. Definitely.'

Eddie Green turned his head from the boat and stared at Kenny. Kenny found himself reddening. 'Phew, ain't it hot?' he said, unconvincingly.

Eddie Green kept staring, saying nothing: and Kenny suddenly flashed the thought that the next thing to happen could be a slap round the face.

'No, Ken.' The man turned back to the boat. 'You're wrong there. This is 'er all right. It's just that you're closer now, see. It's natural it'll look bigger close up than it does out in the water. But this is 'er, mark my words. This is 'ow I saw 'er when you described 'er.' He walked along the quayside above the boat, bending, and peering hard at the battened hatch and the empty wheel-house. 'Empty,' he pronounced. 'Gone off somewhere.' He looked at his watch. 'So. . . .' He stepped on to the deck.

It was immediately obvious he was going to break in. But who could blame him? Kenny thought. After all, instead of being down in Margate with the old lady, for all they knew

125

Patsy could be tied up inside. Or worse! It was only natural he'd want to have a look.

Yeah! A fresh thought struck Kenny. He suddenly brightened. How stupid, not thinking it before. She wouldn't be here, would she? If she'd got this far she'd have gone on by now, if she'd got any sense. Of course! There was still a good chance she'd never know he'd brought Eddie Green after her.

'Oi! What's your game, mate?'

Kenny jumped. Eddie Green swung round, scowling. The stroppy boat owner from further back had followed them along. He was standing by the harbour wall looking down at them suspiciously.

'What's it to you?' Eddie Green stepped back from the deck to the quay, facing up to him like a terrier before a mastiff.

'I've been watching you. You're after something, aren't you?'

'Yeah. That's right, mate, I am. I'm after the bloke who owns this. Not you, is it?' He took another step forward, making his anger obvious.

'No, it isn't me. But I've watched you all the way along, running your eye over everything.' The man stood his ground.

Eddie Green shifted his weight, back to a less aggressive stance. 'You know 'im, then, do you?'

'No.' The man wasn't moving, and he wasn't giving anything away.

'Well, 'e must be up round the town somewhere.' Eddie Green turned to Kenny. 'We'll 'ave a look round the town an' come back later.'

The man said nothing; but still he didn't budge. It was Eddie Green who moved—past Kenny, past the man, and back on to the street.

'Come on,' he said quietly, we're nearly 'ome an' dry. An hour or so won't make much odds. We don't want the law

126

involved. . . .' Kenny shuffled after him. The thought of a walk round the town just now didn't appeal to him at all; although he could see that any move away from the boat had to be a good one. But Eddie Green must have been suffering a bit, too, because he suddenly said, 'Tell you what, I'll 'ave a sit in that boozer, an' you can 'ave a bit of a swim: 'ow about that? You got pants on, 'aven't you?'

'Yeah.' Well, that sounded all right, Kenny thought. An hour in the water . . . and perhaps an hour more for Patsy, on the run.

They walked away from the boat; and very reluctantly the other man turned away. But he didn't go far. From now on, for all of them, it was the waiting game.

Eddie Green had kept an eye on the *Dame Sybil* from a safe distance while Kenny swam. Now, cooled again, Kenny was beginning to feel nicely tired. He settled his back into the shade of a flagging wall.

Eddie Green spoke quietly. 'Five more minutes, mate, an' if I don't seen no one, I'm bustin' in. I've give it long enough.'

Kenny opened his eyes. Back to business. Eddie Green definitely wasn't messing with the police. For some special reason he seemed set on doing this on his own.

'Right. You stay 'ere. An' if you see anyone comin' near the boat, leg it over an' make a bloody great fuss. . . .'

Kenny nodded. He could picture that! He sat up and watched Eddie Green walk straight across the road, no pretence. Direct to the boat he went—probably the best way when you thought about it.

Eddie Green stopped. Suddenly he had come face to face with a man in a peaked cap—and his approach had been too direct to pretend he was going anywhere else. Kenny sat up straight as the small man stiffened into agression.

' 'Ere are you the owner of this boat?' Kenny heard him ask in a loud, belligerent voice.

'No, sir, I'm not.'

'I'm looking for the owner.'

'Oh, yes? Well, you'll find him later, sir. He's up in the town somewhere just now.' The man had a distant eye, and he was staring above Eddie Green's head.

'On 'is own, is 'e?'

'Oh, no, sir. He's with the rest of them.'

Kenny moved himself closer.

'And who's the rest of them?' Eddie Green's urgent questioning was direct, almost like the police himself.

'I don't know. Young people. A couple of fellows and a couple of girls. . . .'

'Girls? 'Ow old?'

The man laughed. 'Old enough to know better, you could say. . . .'

'Big girls?' Eddie Green demonstrated what he meant with his hands.

'Yes, big enough.' The man laughed again. 'Oh, and a youngster. Pretty little thing.'

'Pink dress, short sleeves, fair hair? About so 'igh?'

'Yes, you've got it, sir.'

'An' she's with 'em. Up in the town?'

'That's right, sir. Saw them go this morning. Happy as a bunch of skylarks.'

'An' they'll be back later you reckon?'

'Oh, no doubt about that. This is where they sleep. They've paid their harbour dues till tomorrow afternoon.'

' 'Ave they? All right, thanks, mate.'

'No trouble, sir. No trouble at all.'

Eddie Green got back to Kenny. 'Little madam,' he said. 'She's only up in the town with a bunch of layabouts. But she'll be back, 'e reckons. Now, I'll tell you what, you keep an eye on the boat while I 'ave a little wander round the streets. See if I can see 'er. You never know, I might strike lucky. . . .'

Kenny slumped. 'O.K.,' he said. He was trying to make it all look very boring. But his mouth had gone very dry again. Oh, God! he thought: she *was* still here. Stupid kid! Now when she was found, she'd be bound to know just who'd led Eddie Green to her ... right to her.

In the Little Theatre the outside world and its times of day had ceased to exist. There seemed to have been no morning, no afternoon, and no evening—just one long build-up, like an extended slope, towards the performance. And on that slope, very gradually, the mood inside the building had changed from that of the technical rehearsal to the anticipation of the performance to come. Patsy first felt it when the foyer was being cleared of the snack debris, and tables were set up where programmes would be sold: and it built up bit by bit as the auditorium was cleared of ladders and lights, and the cast was asked to take their personal things backstage.

A pile of programmes appeared in the dressing-room for souvenirs: and Patsy's eyes widened when she saw her own name there on a narrow pink slip folded into the duplicated sheet. 'Tracey Brewer ... Patsy Green'. It took her breath for a moment. This was all getting a bit real! she thought. A nervous screw of excitement turned inside her: but there was a certain melancholy, too. Wouldn't it be different if she was enjoying this properly, like the others? With no Eddie Green and no Jason in her life; but with her mum there to see her— her old mum of the Margate days—and Mrs Broadley, who'd be so proud she'd frame that programme, or stick it in her mirror above the mantelpiece.

But all the same, on her own or not, she'd still be doing it soon. Unless Joe turned funny all of a sudden and she made a run for it, she still had to do the play. A shiver twitched across her back, spine to shoulders, and her ears suddenly felt very sensitive, nervous as a roused cat.

'Come on, lovey,' said Jenny, very matter-of-fact, 'let's get you made-up.' And being a bit heavy-handed with the base, she tried to rub some of the tension away.

Everyone went very quiet very suddenly when the dressing-room door opened and the sound of muffled music drifted in. The audience was arriving. Faces tightened, and Patsy's heart quickened. Oh, Lord, it wouldn't be long now. This new dose of strong emotion didn't help her at all. She felt mixed-up enough already.

'I s'pose it's too late to get took ill?'

'Much too late, lovey. The show must go on!'

Patsy tried to smile. At least Joe wasn't hanging about any more. He was busy round at the side of the stage. Still, he hadn't lost his nerve so far, she thought: and he probably wouldn't, all the time things were going smoothly and she was keeping the group happy.

A loud bang on the dressing-room door battered the sensitive air.

'Fifteen minutes to go!' It was an over-keen call boy; one of the local sons.

'Yes, mate, and that's all you'll have,' Bob muttered, 'if you do that again!' Nevertheless, it started a controlled panic, and everyone began to move towards the stage. Nearly there! Patsy swallowed hard. Good luck, girl! she wished herself. Not what you need it for the most: but good luck, anyway.

Really, she could have stayed in the dressing-room for quite a bit longer. The side of the stage was crowded and she wasn't wanted for a long while; but with all the others in the play from the start, she'd have been on her own back there, and thinking too much. So she stood with the rest and waited.

There was a small peep-hole in the hardboard proscenium which they took turns in looking through. Jenny held Patsy up.

It was disappointing, Patsy thought, after all the hard work. There weren't many people there. The audience only went back about four rows, and even they weren't full rows, just people grouped in the middle on either side of the gangway. In their short-sleeved shirts, their sun-tops and their blouses, with skins which were white, burning red and brown, they sat talking loudly as they fanned themselves with their programmes.

'Oh, God, the faithful few!' said Bob. 'So who wants to see a play on a hot Sunday night by the sea?'

Pete looked next. 'Not to worry. It's quality that counts, not quantity. That's the beauty of being amateur. You can relax and enjoy it.' He turned to Patsy. 'Enjoyment communicates itself, it's infectious. . . .'

And what about being scared stiff? she thought. But she found a smile for him. 'Yeah, I'll do my best,' she said.

Joe ran back across the stage to his desk in the wings—and Patsy saw that he was fully made-up as the murder victim. 'Any minute now,' he said. 'Anyone want a nip?' Where he'd had a screwdriver in his hand one second, now he had a small flask of brandy.

Most heads shook silently; but Bob took a swig. 'Down the hatch,' he said. 'I've got a feeling I might need that.'

'All right, off we go. Good luck.' Joe walked on to the set with Ruth, where they took up their opening positions, ready for the quarrel.

Jenny squeezed Patsy's shoulder. 'This is it, lovey. Be brilliant!'

Just a swallow. Somehow, it was all Patsy could manage.

The auditorium music was fading, and judging by the sudden drop in the talking, Patsy guessed the lights were going down, too. The stage curtains gave a nervous twitch. Oh God, this *was* it. It all had to happen, Patsy thought. Brilliant or rotten, there was nothing could stop her going out there now.

Getting to Mrs Broadley suddenly became a side issue. For the next hour, this was what she had to think about. She shivered in the heat of the dark wings, and looked at Joe through the window in the set. He was standing there, half-turned towards her, ready to swing into the quarrel as soon as the curtains opened.

It struck her now that he'd faded a bit since dinner time. He'd been too busy all the afternoon to pay much attention to her—or so it had seemed. And she'd felt better for it: more independent: more the boss of what she did.

Loud voices. Suddenly, the stage quarrel had begun. The curtains were open and the two of them were going at it hammer and tongs again.

Patsy wasn't giving much thought to it now, but there were some clever lines in the first scene, funny lines thrown in about old quarrels between the husband and the wife; they'd got some good laughs during the dress rehearsal. From the audience, though, there wasn't a murmur. Everything was received in dead silence, as if the play were a tragedy, rather than a comedy thriller.

'God, that looks like hard work out there,' Bob whispered. 'They're not laughing at a thing! Not much sense of humour down this way....'

The others looked out on to the set where Ruth and Joe were posturing, threatening, suddenly drawing back, delivering the lines with machine-gun devastation.

'Let's just hope they go for the sinister stuff....'

Bob walked round to the other side of the set for his entrance, and Jenny looked in through the window with Patsy. 'Oh well, lovey,' she said, 'at least we've got the weather and the boat....'

At last Joe came off, perspiring. 'They're a bit quiet,' he said, disappointed. 'Hardly worth all the effort.' Patsy could tell that he was trying to apologize to anyone within earshot for wasting all their time, bringing them all this way for such a poor reception. 'Anyway, Patsy, you've got nothing to lose. After this I think I'll need a stage name to go under, the same as you....'

Patsy looked at him in his overdone make-up. The idiot! He might be upset, but saying something stupid like that, even muttering it, could give the whole thing away for her.

Why was it some grown-ups said such stupid things at times? He was supposed to be on her side.

All thoughts of the play faded then, and thoughts of being sent back to Eddie Green dominated Patsy's mind. What was he doing tonight? she wondered. Was he searching like mad for her, because it was looking bad for him, her going? Or was he sitting in his armchair, watching the telly and not caring a damn if he never saw her again?

'Come on, be lucky!' Jenny suddenly said. 'We're nearly on!'

'Yeah.' She'd been stupid, letting her mind wander like that. She'd nearly missed it. She took in two or three fluttering, butterfly breaths. Before she knew it, Jenny was gone. She was on, and her voice ringing round the hall. Patsy waited. Then out of nowhere her cue came. No, not yet! she thought. They'd cut a chunk out, hadn't they?

Without thinking she pushed herself on to the stage. She walked out to where she'd been told to stand. There was a sudden silence. Bob had just said something, she was aware of that, and then there was the silence. Hold on! Was it down to her so quick? Help, what did she have to say? Her spotlight was on. At least she was remembering to look into that. But thinking about the spotlight was only one of the different levels she'd been on before. Before she'd been Tracey, with Patsy watching what she was doing. She could even remember that. But now, God help her, she was only Patsy. She wasn't Tracey at all. She wasn't acting. She wasn't anything....

Patsy froze solid. All at once her mind was as void as boundless snow. She was struck rigid. She couldn't move: not her legs, and not her mouth. She had words to say, but she hadn't the first idea what they were. Wasn't she supposed to be Jenny's little girl? Yes, she was—and now she couldn't even remember her name....

Bob said something again; but Patsy couldn't understand him. He might just as well have been speaking double Dutch. A voice from backstage said something. Were they trying to help her? Yes, she was being prompted; she was supposed to pick it up from there. But it all meant nothing. Nothing of any of it seemed to be connected with anything that was going on in her mind. All she was conscious of now was that bright spotlight, shining into her eyes. Her brain seemed to have

133

stopped working. It wasn't picking anything up. A muscle behind her knee was twitching, and her legs were starting to shake. She could see these people on the stage, all staring at her, sweating, trying to keep their faces straight, looking horror at her out of their eyes.

Bob asked her another question. His voice had gone up higher. He was trying to lead her in again. But Patsy had gone completely. There was nothing in the world she could do till those curtains closed. Please God, let the curtains close. . . .

She heard one remark. It came from the audience. An old girl with a loud voice. 'Poor little duck,' she said.

Jenny fumbled back through the door, and tripping over the words, she tried to tell the detective what Tracey was supposed to have seen. Patsy even recognized some of it. But she knew the scene was lost. The audience was murmuring, and as the curtain came across at last it wasn't to a burst of applause, but to a chorus of sympathetic 'aaahs'.

Patsy could hear all that, and she thought she could move now. But she didn't know where to move to. Oh, God, what did you do? Where did you go after something like that?

She felt a hand on her shoulder; a soft hand. 'Never mind, lovey. They're a lousy audience, we all know that. You shouldn't have let it get to you.'

'Come on, Jenny, quick change, short interval,' Bob said as he brushed past.

Pete walked off the stage in silence.

It was Joe who helped most. In the middle of shifting some chairs on the set he came to Patsy with his little flask of brandy. 'Now then, lassie, you're having a tot of this if I have to hold your nose.' She took it, and swigged it. Her eyes filled with red tears and her throat burned: but it gave her sufficient fire to move one foot and then the other, and walk slowly back to the dressing-room.

Waiting had been a curse. It didn't matter how quick people thought they were being, waiting for them was always a long, boring business. It had seemed to Kenny as if Eddie Green had been away all day. All right, he'd done well not dragging Kenny round the town, leaving him there in the shade instead, with his back to a groyne, but after enough people with ice-cream had walked past once and stared at him, and then walked back again with second helpings, Kenny had begun to feel like one of the sights that had been left on the beach to rot. Worst of all, he'd got hungry, and that was bad news when you didn't have any money. Not that he'd done badly for food the day before; Eddie Green had got hungry as well, and he'd taken care of things then; but Kenny's last bit of food that Sunday had been the bacon sandwich, early, and every now and then the juices down below had started fighting and squirting all over nothing.

There'd been a time—it must have been about dinner time—when Kenny had felt like getting up and going; having a shuffle round the streets to see if he could bump into Eddie Green. But the grumblings inside had stopped for a while, and he must have nodded off to sleep, because the next he'd known, Eddie Green had been shaking his shoulder.

'Come on, Ken,' he'd said; 'we'll 'ave a pie an' a pint. . . .'

It had been even later than Kenny had thought, because the pub had been just on closing; but there had been time for two pies and a bag of crisps in the car-park before the glasses got collected.

'God knows where they are,' Eddie Green had moaned. 'There ain't a sign of anyone round the streets. All the shops are shut. Everyone's on the beach—an' they ain't there, I've looked. Probably gone off in the country for the day. But it seems flamin' silly to me, 'aving that boat an' not using it in the good weather. . . .'

On a full stomach, Kenny had slept that afternoon; and he'd woken himself up with another swim in the cool water. And then it had been a quick dry in the sun, and time for ham sandwiches and cups of tea in a café. In between everything else they'd done, though, they'd kept a close eye on the *Dame Sybil*. They'd done nothing for long that had left the boat free of observation from one or other of them.

Altogether it had been a mixed-up day to Kenny; matey at times, but worrying; and Eddie Green could still get very ratty very quickly. 'Christ, they gotta come back some time,' he said now, as both their backsides ached with sitting on the stones. 'It's bloody *evening*.'

Kenny nodded. But it was only for show. Rotten as it was, waiting, his fervent hope was that they never did come back— or that if they did, it turned out that Patsy had already made her break for Margate. As far as he could see that was the only chance he had of coming out of this with any respect. . . .

Lumped-up with misery, Patsy sat on her chair and stared into the mirror. She stared until she could only see her eyes, until the rest of her face was nothing but a stranger's blur, and on her own with her disappointment she wallowed in what might have been. It was just what she did in the small bedroom in Deptford, every time the wet sheets had been found again.

It was always *your* fault, that was the trouble. No one else had done it, had they? It was always down to you: you plus your luck, or God, or your stars, or whatever it was worked everything out.

She focussed her eyes on her wretched face. 'You silly cow,' she muttered to herself. 'There wasn't no call for that.'

The rest were on the stage, doing the second act. Well, it was a good job she wasn't in that! They wouldn't have let her near. Not that anyone had said a lot. Just Jenny. 'Don't worry,' she'd smiled, 'it'll all be forgotten before you know it;' but that was all.

So, what was she going to do next, then? One thing was certain: Joe wasn't going to bother to keep her secret any more: not if the group hadn't got any more use for her. When they said she'd better go home, he'd soon find some way of letting them know. Buy a paper specially, no doubt, and leave it around. . . . In which case her best bet right now was out the back way while they were all busy in there, and up to the main road for Margate. . . .

Right! Suddenly, she found she'd made her mind up. After all the worrying since last night, this mess-up had decided it for her. She was going. And she was going now. She'd just have to get this make-up off her face first—Mrs Broadley wouldn't want to see some little madam at her front door— and then it was away.

Patsy dipped her fingers in the make-up remover and smeared it vigorously over her face. She scrubbed at herself with a handful of disintegrating tissue. Come on! she urged herself. Quick! Before someone comes in and tries to stop you! Now that she'd made her mind up, she really had to move. There wouldn't be any other chances. God, she looked a right creamy mess! She found someone's towel and finished off, leaving orange on it, and she ran a greasy comb through her hair. Right. Now, money. She'd need some money to catch a bus, wouldn't she?

Jenny's handbag lay open on the dressing-room table. Patsy's fingers dipped.

'I wouldn't do that if I was you. . . .'

Patsy didn't turn. By now she knew the voice too well. Oh, God, no! Not him again. She felt physically sick, wanted to throw up.

'Don't be daft, girl,' Joe said. 'That's not going to solve anything, is it?'

Patsy said nothing; she just shrugged, defiantly.

'Oh, come on, Patsy, you don't want to let it get to you. For goodness sake stop worrying about what happened. Listen, do you think you're the first one of this lot who's made a mess of a scene on the stage?' Joe sat down on a handy chair, back to front. 'They've all done it, one time or another. Everyone has. Famous actors and actresses wouldn't have anything to put in their autobiographies if they hadn't made a few ghastly mistakes in their time. Haven't you ever seen those things they show on the television? All the mistakes, put together for a laugh? Come on, sweetheart, cheer up! They'll all be pulling your leg about it tomorrow.' He felt for his pipe, but he hadn't got it with him. 'And you won't freeze up like that in Herne Bay, I can tell you. It never happens twice.'

Patsy's face was closed. But, why was he being so nice? she was thinking. She couldn't understand it. Not when she'd just put the tin lid on his trip down here.

'Look, I've got to go. They'll be ready for the pistol shot soon. But I just thought I'd try to cheer you up....'

'Yeah. Thanks.'

He looked as if he really was going; but he hesitated; there was something else he wanted to say. Patsy prepared herself for it. Was he going to say he'd have to end the deal now?

'Trust me, Patsy,' he said. 'I won't let you down, love....'

And he went. Quite choked, he'd sounded. What did he mean with all that? Patsy sat down again. Strewth, how things changed! Now she didn't know where to start thinking about everything. She'd been going just then ... and now ... well now, her body began to feel drained, exhausted, and strangely calm, almost as if she'd taken a couple of aspirin.

For three crucial minutes she stayed where she was: and then the chance to go had disappeared as people started running in and out, quick-changing—still moaning about the dreadful audience. From then on someone or other was about all the time, except for the couple of minutes it took them to take their curtain call, and she let it go at that, sitting there unmoved, watching them winding down, and not even knowing whether or not she wanted the chance to go any more. Suddenly all that was past her. Now all she had to do was somehow get through the unwelcome celebration party and find the quietness of a night in bed where she could lie still and sort her thinking out.

Patsy sat and watched as the drink soaked into the general depression. There was no real laughter, nothing genuinely relaxed: instead, a lot of noise and brittle gaiety. By one o'clock they felt they could decently go. With a few muted good-byes the group gathered up their bags and walked out into the cool night air. The streets were quiet now, and the boat, too. Patsy deliberately kept herself well out of everybody's way: she was first down the steps, first into bed, and she quickly turned her face to the bulkhead, pretending instant sleep. The least said just now, she thought, the soonest mended. It was a lesson she'd learned from two years with Eddie Green. But in the watching, and the walking, she'd thought out what she was going to do. If Joe kept his word, and his mouth shut, she would go with them on the boat to Herne Bay next day: and only when the moment was right, was she going to make her break. One thing she was very clear about once again was her goal. Stuff the play. Now it was Mrs Broadley tomorrow, or nothing. . . .

Kenny was awake, too, listening to the gentle shift of the shingle down on the beach. It had all gone really wrong now, he thought. If only he'd let Eddie Green lead the way home to Deptford that morning there'd be no Patsy to face when she came back to the boat. But no, he'd fancied another day out with the man, maybe another camp fire to share—and all it had led to was this: the two of them booked into a small room at the top of this pub, and Eddie Green down by the harbour keeping watch on the *Dame Sybil* from the middle of a stack of corporation deck chairs. And it had been a rotten day, really. It hadn't lived up to any of his expectations. Once the bus had got them here it had been all walking, and watching, and waiting, with just the short swims in between: nothing special: no more talking together about things. Just waiting awake in different places for Patsy and her funny friends to come back.

The man in the peaked cap had told them in the end. 'Very late, they were before, sir. One or two. I wouldn't wait up for them if I was you. Catch them in the morning, before the tide. . . .' But Eddie Green wasn't going to trust them not to slip out on the tail-end of the evening ebb. To make sure, he'd shifted some chairs to form a shelter, set one of them in the middle of the den, and sat down to wait. He'd told the guv'nor at the Anchor his hard luck story and got a better reception than he had the night before: even a key during the evening, when he'd returned for a warming brandy. Then he'd gone back to keep watch. 'I'll see you later,' he'd said, 'when I know that boats on the mud can't get out. Then we'll 'ave 'em in the morning.'

Kenny looked around the poky room. God, it was peculiar, in a strange bed in someone's pub. The haystack had been a million times better.

He sighed and looked out of the window at the sky. There were no stars out tonight. That seemed strange. It was as if they'd all been switched off, like the end of a season of illuminations. No coloured stars, no meteorites. Nothing any more to make him feel good. . . .

Kenny forced his eyes closed. It wouldn't be so bad if he could get off: then the next thing he'd know would be morning, and everything could be sorted out in the daylight. It'd looked different to everybody tomorrow. But it wasn't easy to sleep the wait away. Just for now, his conscience wouldn't give in that easily. . . .

It was Bob who suggested it. He looked a bit sloshed, Patsy thought, but after what had happened she couldn't say his idea was right out of order. Of course, it was late, but nobody was asleep, and when Bob said it no one disagreed with him.

'Look, you can all go off to sleep and ignore it if you like:

but I say that was a right fiasco tonight. She came on that stage and never said a word, right?'

They all looked at Patsy; and they all nodded.

'And that's not being unfair to the little lady, is it, Uncle Joe?'

Joe stopped fiddling with his pipe and looked up. 'No,' he said, 'mind, you've all made a hash of things at some time or another. But tonight, all right, we'll have to agree it was down to Patsy.' He went back to shredding an evening newspaper and filling the pipe's bowl with it.

Patsy sat on her bunk and wondered what was coming next.

'Well, all right, then,' Bob went on. 'Now, we're supposed to be doing this rubbish in Herne Bay again tomorrow, and we do need to be a little bit certain the same thing's not going to happen, don't we? You follow me? We've either got to be sure she's up to it, or someone'll have to read her lines from backstage.'

Joe nodded his agreement.

'So what are you suggesting?' Jenny asked, her voice just this side of being rude.

'Obvious. Do the scene again, in front of a few people. She did it all right yesterday morning, and she did it all right at the rehearsal. But she froze solid when she came to do it in front of the audience. So, if she's going to do it again, she's got to prove she can do it with people watching....'

But there *were* people watching at the rehearsal, Patsy thought. There were people there who clapped. She said nothing, though. She was beginning to feel uncomfortable in another way. Let him have his say, then when they started talking about something else she'd quietly slip into the lavatory....

Pete suddenly joined in. 'Well, that's no problem. Something can be arranged. Now shut up, Bob, and let's all get some sleep, for God's sake.'

Patsy suddenly felt more cheerful. At least Pete hadn't written her off.

'But there won't be time tomorrow, Pete. I've worked it out.' Bob smeared a handful of make-up remover on to his face, circling it as he talked. 'Look, we're putting it on in Herne Bay tomorrow night. By the time we get out of here on the tide we're not going to have time to do much more than unload the van and set up. There's no rehearsal time, you know that.'

Pete twisted his mouth in thought. He looked at the narrow pink programme slip with Patsy's name on it, as if the information were shown there. 'Yes,' he said, 'that's true. So what's your big idea?'

'Easy. We just go up on deck and do it now. We find a few people along the front to sit and watch, and let them be the audience. Only I don't want to find myself stuck on that stage again, standing there like some sort of idiot while nothing happens.'

They all murmured their agreement, even Jenny: and Patsy couldn't help seeing the fairness in it. But quite honestly right now she'd feel a bit easier, if she could just slip along to the little lavatory by the steps. After that she'd go through her scene as many times as they wanted. She knew she knew it: and she knew she'd never freeze on it ever again.

'What about her note? The permission?' Joe asked, still shredding paper into his pipe. 'She'll need that to do it again.'

'No problem,' said Bob. He held up the sheet of Basildon Bond from Patsy's kitchen drawer. 'I've got it here.'

'Come on, then,' Jenny said. 'Let's get it over with, lovey.'

With the look of someone who was out to prove something, Bob led the way on to the deck.

'Here, hold on,' Patsy heard herself saying. 'Just a minute. I just want to. . . .'

'Oh, come on, no time like the present,' Jenny said. 'Let's show miserable Bob. . . .' and she gently propelled Patsy ahead of her up the steep steps. Patsy protested.

'Come on, lovey, this won't take two ticks. Let's get this over with and back to bed. . . .'

They went up into the night. It was clear, without a moon,

just a sprinkling of bright stars, and now, despite her discomfort, Patsy couldn't help wondering at the clarity of their colours—a red star, low on the horizon, and an azure blue above her. She stared at the depth of the sky. It was beautiful, she thought, like nothing she'd ever seen from the smoky flats in Deptford, or from the roof of the old school.

'So, where's the audience?' Ruth wanted to know.

'Use your eyes,' said Bob, 'look over there.'

Patsy followed Bob's arm to the quayside, where there seemed to be people sitting near a pile of deck-chairs. She squinted, but she couldn't make out who was there. She didn't care a lot, either: because what was suddenly urgent at that moment was a dive back down those steps to the lavatory. There'd definitely be no acting from her till she'd been. She'd tried to tell them that. And it wouldn't take a minute. She went over to Bob, who was splashing his feet in the water again.

'Won't be a minute,' she said. 'You do your bit with Pete. I'll be back before you get to me.'

'You'd better, young lady.'

Patsy ignored that; but before she could move for the steps a strong white beam swung full into her face. Her spotlight! It was so bright it hurt her eyes. For a moment she couldn't see a thing. 'Hold on! Wait! Turn it off a minute, I've gotta go,' she called. In her blindness she groped for the wheel-house. It was terrible, not seeing; it was like calling out and not making a sound; or running away, and not moving. In her darkness she felt wide open to attack, as if anyone could grab her without her knowing they were coming. Eddie Green. . . .

She turned, and turned, and fumbled about: the handrail!

Quick! After all this stupid mucking about she was only just going to make it. Holding her muscles tight, she slid herself quickly down the steps, and in the relief of the soft cabin lights she saw the lavatory door and made a grab at it. Inside! Just time to lock it. There! And, oh, thank God. . . .

And then, rigid, knowing—as she always knew at this

143

moment—Patsy woke. Like a hundred times before she woke to the shameful warmth of a wet bed.

Oh, no! That terrible trick had been played on her again: that trick dream where everything seems real, where you're doing everything right, in the right place—but where you're not really. Where you think you're in the lavatory, but you're really wetting the bed. Where you always find out five seconds too late to stop.

Patsy lay there on her bunk, her heart thumping hard inside the thinness of her ribs. It was all right for a minute, but very soon every move would be in cold guilt.

The dream was still there in her head, and then it would go. All the mix-ups which had been so real just now had been only the cunning twists of her brain: Joe, filling his pipe with the evening paper she'd been worried about; Bob calling him 'Uncle Joe'; Pete reading the tide times off the programme slip; the bright coloured stars; and the spotlight up there on the side of the harbour. She'd taken it all as normal in her sleep.

And all at once the anger and the disappointment of doing it again rose up inside her and gorged in her throat. It wasn't her *fault*, was it? Not if she didn't mean to do it? It was God, or Eddie Green, who kept making her do it. . . .

Oh, mum, but they'd hate her for this, wouldn't they? This toffy lot. There weren't any rubbers on these bunks, so it would have gone through, into the mattress, where people sat in the day-time. Now they were going to have a worse reason for not liking Patsy Bligh than her freezing up on the stage.

Right! That was it. She was going then. She wasn't going to sit and listen to all their whispers all the way round to Herne Bay. No, she was clearing off. And double-quick, too!

Patsy shifted, lifted to look out of the porthole. Already she felt clammy and uncomfortable, with her pyjamas gripping wetly round her legs, like cold seaweed. From the gloom of the cabin the sky had that look of filling up with light, definitely morning. Around her were the hummocks of sleep. It would be easy to leave this: there'd be no pangs at getting away from these unfriendly twists in the bedclothes.

As quietly as she could, Patsy wriggled out of the sheets. Sliding hold of her Co-op bag, she padded silently along to the lavatory. People did get out before they got up, so no one would take much notice of her, even if they should happen to turn over. But she didn't want to make any more noise than she could help. She used a towel, rather than running the water, and she found her clean change. Quickly, in the cramped quarters, she dressed and finger-combed her hair. She stepped into her plastic sandals and then stood; waiting; listening to the sounds of sleep. Now, she had to be sure for this next bit. What she didn't want was someone seeing her go up those steps into the open.

She held her breath to listen better. There were the same murmurs she'd heard before, and one whining snore: but nothing else: there didn't seem to be any moving about, or talking.

She jabbed the door open, and then held it firm. Slow doors creaked loudest, she'd learned that the hard way. She waited. Still nothing. Still the same hummocks. O.K. Leaving the bag behind, she eased round to the steps and almost slid up them in a single move of silent hurry. As she knew it would be, the wheel-house door was open—and all at once, in the cool of a fresh day, she found herself on the *Dame Sybil*'s deck and jumping off on to the Steeple Stones hard.

The secret was out now. As soon as they woke they'd know she'd run off. They'd know it because she wasn't there, and because of what was left behind. And then, Joe or not, the truth would come out. So it was a race. Patsy to Mrs Broadley's, or this lot and the police to her. The trouble was, she didn't know for sure how far she'd got to go—and she couldn't even guess at what she might meet up with on the way.

Already, as she left the boat, a headache began to press into the top of her head, like some giant thumb at work. Worry, she told herself; all her troubles, the same thing her mum was always saying. But it was horrible; and if she was her mum, she thought, she'd hate having this rotten feeling all the time.

Patsy looked round carefully, her eye drawn especially to the deck-chairs of her recent dream. But there was no one there, of course—no audience to test her out. It was stupid, the tricks that dreams played. She turned away. She didn't want to hang about. It was hard to tell what time it was, the sun was a bit hazed-over today, but she'd got to get a good start on the others before they all woke up and started chasing round after her. She squinted up at the sky again. Yes, it was definitely different today. It wasn't going to be so sunny. But then that was nothing, was it? That wasn't going to stop her getting on.

Patsy had a good idea which way to go. All she had to do was head away from the sea and she was bound to come to the red road on the map that led to Margate. Up past the theatre and keep carrying on. She knew she couldn't miss it, if she kept the sea at her back.

There was no one about. What day was it? Sunday, Monday? Anyway, whatever day it was, it must still be early: there were empty milk bottles on the doorsteps. She was even ahead of the milkman. She hurried on. The little roads, dead in their sleep, seemed endless and unfriendly. All those families asleep in all those bedrooms, she thought. All together. Suddenly, it made her feel lonely; and, thinking about it as she hurried on, she realized that although she'd been running away from home she'd been with other people all the time. Up to now. She'd been on her own for a time in the dressing-room, and on the boat, but there'd been other people around her. Now she was on the run completely by herself. And she didn't like it. Not a bit. A mate, she could have done with Mary McArthy. Or even Kenny Granger, if he could have kept up with her.

She started to run. The sooner she got to that main road the better she'd feel. At least she'd feel she was on her way then.

That main road led to Margate, and Margate meant Mrs Broadley. But all these little roads were just a lot of fiddling about: she hadn't really got anywhere yet. Her sandals flapped on the pavement, and she tried to run faster to leave the sound behind.

Straight over this road and up to the top, she decided. It looked like it was wider up there. A bigger road, more main, it probably led up to the one she wanted. She took a quick look left, and right, nothing coming, then over ... and....

'Good morning, young lady. In a bit of a hurry, aren't we?'

Oh, God, no! Her inside turned over. Next worse to Eddie Green! A rotten policeman!

''Ello. Yeah! 'Scuse me, I'm ever so late....'

'Yes, it looks like it.' He had her arm: not hurting, but firm. 'So where are you off to, this early in the morning?'

She didn't even have to think about it. It just came, straight out, and sure. 'Paper round. Leave off, I'll get killed, being late....'

The policeman's grip slackened just a little.

'Oh, and which shop would that be?'

'The big one. Up the station.'

'Ah.'

'Please ... he said I'll lose the round for good if I'm late again.'

'Did he?' The policeman stared at her; then he softened into an understanding smile. 'All right. Far be it from me to lose anyone their job.' He let go altogether. 'But aren't you a bit young to be doing a paper round?'

'No! Dunno. You'll 'ave to come up the shop and talk to the man....'

'Yes.... All right, perhaps I will at that. Anyway, you get on, I haven't seen you....'

Looking considerate, he stood aside and Patsy ran. She put her head down and went, like on Sports Day, out of his sight as quickly as her legs and her lungs could take her. Her feet slap-slapped on the pavement like a simple sort of engine.

That had been a bit of luck: her answer, coming like that, so quick! Must have been the way her thoughts went: policeman, people looking for her, being in the papers, paper round. Something like that. . . .

She ran on with her mouth tasting bitter and her headache pounding in time to her feet.

. . . And of course, she'd known from that map there was a railway line somewhere near; she'd been going on it the other night; so it was a safe bet there'd be a paper shop near a station. Anyway, who cared, the Old Bill had swallowed it all right. In spite of all her problems, she felt quite proud of herself again, like when she'd got rid of the stop press column in the theatre.

Across roads she went, along by people's walls, brushing on their privet to keep herself in and be as inconspicuous as possible.

Yes, and here it was, Patsy thought—a paper shop. It could be the one she'd imagined. But even as she looked in self-congratulation at the closed door, she saw the notice . . . and all at once her legs felt drained of energy, and her stomach suddenly wormed with a new turn of panic. Oh, no!

DISPUTE—NO PAPERS
OPEN 10—12 ONLY

Paper Dispute. How long before that copper tumbled to it?

Within strides now, though her body had had enough, she wanted to walk, to stop and gather her strength: but she pushed herself to run on and on until she was almost running on the spot. Wasn't she ever going to get to the blessed road? They'd been short roads down by the harbour, but they were getting longer and longer; and there were fields, and a cemetery, and posh houses. Everything was spreading out, as if what she was after was moving away from her all the time in a bad dream. Wasn't it ever going to come, the Thanet Way? Or had she missed it? Please God, she had to find it quick, she *had* to: and then there were no two ways about it, she had to bunk a lift. It was urgent. She couldn't stay round here for long. That copper was going to cotton any minute: and then he'd start thinking. . . .

Time was running out, real fast.

12

Witnessing a serious argument always upset Kenny. His belly churned and his throat tightened at the sight and the sound of two people arguing the toss. Perhaps it was because grown-ups arguing sounded much the same as kids quarrelling—and that always hit home at Kenny. There was no need for grown-ups to descend to that level. He'd also found that being close to a big bust-up usually meant you got roped into it, and that was even less clever. He'd dreaded this happening, anyway, so he stood well back when Eddie Green started shouting the odds on the deck of the *Dame Sybil*.

It had all begun below, out of sight. Running straight from the pub, Eddie Green had sent himself down through the open doorway of the wheel-house like a whippet down a rabbit hole: and minutes later everyone had come up as if they'd been flushed out. First, two women, looking frightened, and then three men, sounding as if they were only just managing to persuade Eddie Green to say it all up there before he killed them in their beds.

'Are you tryin' to tell me I said you could take 'er?' he was shouting. 'What stroke d'you call that?'

Everyone was falling over themselves trying to answer Eddie Green at the same time. And they were all trying to sound very reasonable.

'. . . It said she could come. . . .'

'. . . she said she'd asked you. . . .'

'. . . it would help while your son was in hospital. . . .'

But Eddie Green was in a real fighting mood. 'My boy's as right as ninepence,' he shouted. 'Never 'ad a day's illness in 'is life. What's up with you? You call yourselves brainy? Taking a kid off on a boat miles away and not checking with no one first? You go on a kid's say-so?'

'There wasn't any time. We'd have missed the tide. . . .'

'Stuff the tide!' Eddie Green stood back a pace; he looked as if he were measuring himself for throwing a punch.

'But we had your written permission.'

Eddie Green twisted himself away. His angry face showed what he thought of such a diabolical lie. Kenny thought he was going to explode—or kill someone in his outrage.

'You stupid. . . .'

'Look. You did write this, didn't you? This isn't a child's handwriting. It's not taught like this any more.'

One of the women was standing there thrusting a piece of paper at Eddie Green.

Eddie Green was forced to read it. For a second he put it away from him, down at his side while he looked at the sky, as if he couldn't believe what it said: then he looked at it again, and he started spluttering. 'But . . . God give me bloody strength . . . this weren't for you . . . you berks . . . this was for the flaming school!'

Now the shocked looks were being shot between the others.

'This was wrote for 'er school outing!' Eddie Green shouted. 'Some trip down Kent she was pestering for. You show me where it says about going on some flaming boat!'

Kenny saw the tall dark-haired man take the paper and read it, while Eddie Green stood there with his hands on his hips glaring at him.

'Actually, it fits either way,' the man said calmly, sounding as if nothing ever threw him for long. 'She told us you were going to the hospital every day to see your son, and we thought we were doing you a favour by giving her a holiday. She gave us your note, which seemed reasonable enough. Given those circumstances, you can't blame us for reading what we did into it. You read it that way. *We* were coming to Kent, too, on *our* sort of tour: a theatrical tour. All this could have applied to us.' He hit the piece of paper with his fingers.

Eddie Green turned away and stared out at the estuary again. Was he counting to ten to cool down—or was he poising himself to swing back suddenly and lay one on the bloke?

'You see, she was in our play: she played a small part,' the tall man said. 'We even put her name in the programme. We weren't trying to keep anything secret you know. . . .'

'What name?' Eddie Green had turned back. His voice was low and wary.

'Her name, of course. Your name. Patsy Green. That's right, isn't it?'

There was a long silence. Then all at once, the fight seemed to have gone from Eddie Green, like it does from a dog when the cat's owner comes out. 'It's as near as makes no odds,' he said.

Everyone stood very still.

Anyway, where *was* Patsy? Kenny wondered. Was she still in the boat, left down there in disgrace? Or had she gone—made her break for Margate? Now this tension had eased he was back to worrying about Patsy and him again.

'So where is she now?' Eddie Green asked abruptly: he looked around, almost as if he expected her to come walking back along the front with a morning paper for someone.

'She's gone,' one of the women told him. 'She had a little accident in the night . . . you know . . . and when we woke up, she'd gone. . . .'

'Run off again,' the man with the fair hair added.

It was in that instant that Kenny felt sorry for Eddie Green. He'd never thought he could—but right now he'd never seen anyone look so . . . well, beaten, was the only word for it.

The man looked all round, very slowly, like someone taking in the news of a family death. He looked lost. At last his eyes fixed on Kenny, and he shrugged his shoulders hopelessly. Kenny stared down at the ground. The next words would be the words of someone giving in.

'Then we'll bloody find 'er!' Eddie Green told the harbour

in general. His eyes had lit up. ''Ave to, won't we? Or a missing girl who was on your boat ain't gonna look too clever for you, is it?'

'No ... well....' It was the older man, who hadn't said anything so far, just watched from the wheel-house door. 'Well, look, what I suggest is, we go below and work out some sort of a plan.'

To Kenny's surprise, Eddie Green quickly agreed to go back into the boat again. He stepped over the deck to the wheel-house. Before he went below, though, he remembered Kenny on the quay. 'You come along of us,' he called. ''E's 'elping me,' he said. 'Come on, you're in this....'

While they all looked at him with the old looks, Kenny shuffled over to the tilt of the deck. Dead right, he thought. I am in it. Right up to there!

But it seemed out of order, somehow, going down into the boat where Patsy had been living: like going into her bedroom, or talking about her to her mum, when she wasn't there. Worse than that, though, the steep steps down into the cabin hadn't been made for people of Kenny's size, and after the embarrassment of getting below, the whole idea of the boat felt alien. And none of them seemed to know what to make of him. A side-kick, a hanger-on, what part did the fat boy have in all this? their frowns seemed to ask. They didn't draw him into the conversation, and they only offered him a cup of coffee as an afterthought. While for the rest of the time, he was left to sit round-backed on one of the bunks and see off the usual God-what-a-size! sidelong glances with frowns of his own.

Eddie Green didn't give much away. Kenny noticed that. He didn't tell them about Patsy at home, and all that bother. Instead, he kept asking them questions about what she'd told them, and about anything she'd let out or done to give a clue about what was in her mind. He heard about the play— nodding impatiently at all their acting rubbish—but his attitude changed abruptly when one of the women reached

153

over and brought out a folded-up map from a narrow shelf.

'I'll tell you something, for what it's worth,' the woman said. 'Now I think about it, she was taking rather a lot of interest in where we were yesterday. And this ...' she unfolded the map, '... this road to Margate kept her quite preoccupied for a while. She kept asking me about distances. . . .'

'Ah!' Joe reached for the map. 'I wondered who'd folded this back on itself. You can always tell. . . .'

But Eddie Green was off his edge of bunk and stubbing a bitten fingernail anxiously along the crinkles of the Ordnance Survey. 'Margate?' he asked. 'Looking at Margate, was she?'

'Well, Margate was mentioned. . . .'

'Yeah ... I bet. . . .' But Eddie Green said no more. He just seemed to become more and more generally agitated, impatient to move.

The older man started refolding the map. 'Well, if it's Margate you want we can certainly get you along there,' he said. 'The boat's held up by the tide for a bit, that's all. . . .'

'It's the police you need, if you ask me,' the man with fair hair said.

But Eddie Green jumped on that almost before he'd finished saying it. 'No, leave them out,' he said. The older man nodded agreement. 'If she's gone by the road then we'll go that way an' all. She won't've got far, I don't suppose. We'll find a taxi, me an' the boy. . . .'

The golden girl flashed her eyes. She hadn't said very much so far: but now her face said she thought Eddie Green was stupid. 'How the hell are you going to find her in the whole of Margate?' she asked. 'She might have got there by now—and it's a pretty big place on a Bank Holiday, you know.'

'Yeah, I know. You leave that to me,' Eddie Green growled. 'She won't be very far from 'Dreamland'. Never fret, I know where she'll be.' He looked at Kenny; and Kenny looked at the matting on the floor. 'I reckon we both know where she'll be, don't we, son? Eh?'

Kenny had to nod his head. There was nothing else he could do. Eddie Green had got him.

'Well anyway, I'll get transport for you.' The older man stood up quickly. 'I've got a pal with a car. I'll come with you—get you where you want to go pretty quick.' And in two or three strides, belying his age, he was up the steps and striding away across the deck.

There was no mistaking the road when she got to it. Patsy knew without any doubt that it was that main red road, running along to Margate. Even this early it was busy; not nose-to-tail yet, there were gaps; but it was flowing. Looking at it, Patsy could see that most of it was family stuff, cars with four or five people in them making an early start for the best places on the sand. Of course, there were no coaches this early; they wouldn't be down from London for a bit; but there were various vans and lorries rattling about their business already.

Patsy stood watching them go by from the wide grass verge. There was still a dew on the grass, and a haze of mist hung above the hedges. It was a bit cold, too, but after so many fantastic days of weather, who was going to imagine this one could be any different? Anyway, Patsy wasn't bothered about the weather. Get out of here, that was all she had to do. And quick!—before that copper had a car out here to pick her up. The big trouble was, how? She had to have a lift, she'd known that a long time, but now she was here, who could she thumb? If she stopped one of these family cars they'd have her down at the nearest nick before she could say Eddie Green.

She was keeping herself well back in a small gateway; she reckoned she'd be all right here for a few minutes while she thought about it. They'd think she was some country kid waiting for her dad on his tractor. But she couldn't stay here for ever. *She had to get away.*

And if it wasn't a family, if it was someone on their own, she'd be taking a big chance, wouldn't she? What about finding herself in a car with one of those barmies—like the bloke by the creek; or with someone like Joe, where she didn't know for sure what he was up to?

But all the same, *she had to get away*. Any second now and the next car up this road was going to be the Old Bill. And then it'd be too late. All that terrible aggravation up to now would have been for nothing.

Two women drove past in a Volkswagen. Sisters, Patsy thought; or two teachers; both talking at once. Well, what about a lift from a woman, then? You stood a better chance trusting a woman . . . didn't you?

The road where Patsy stood was on an incline. It wasn't much of a slope—only the big stuff and the old bangers were seriously slowed down by it—but it was giving her time to see how many people were in each vehicle, and whether the drivers were men or women. That was a help. Trying to look nonchalant, but keeping her eyes sharp, she stared at one vehicle after another as they drove up past her. But nothing promising came up for ages; and a breathless feeling of panic was just beginning to rise up inside her, impelling her to start making a move away on foot, when chugging up the slope there came a dark blue, dusty van stacked up in the back with trays of eggs; and at the wheel, on her own, was a woman; scruffy and preoccupied, peering out through the windscreen with a frown. God! Just the job! Patsy thought. And just in the nick of time. . . .

Impulsively, Patsy ran out across the wet verge and hung over the kerb, anxiously waving her arms, looking a bit as if she'd found a body behind the hedge. 'Hey!' she called. 'Please. . . .' But to her disgust and disappointment the van just went chugging on. The woman looked neither to left nor to right through her dirty glasses.

'Stupid old cow!' Patsy shouted. But a big lorry was rumbling up immediately behind, and Patsy turned her back on the road and made a dash for the gateway. God, though! Some people wouldn't see a million pounds if you dangled it in front of their stupid, long noses.

156

A sudden hiss of air brakes shot a bird out of the hedge in a flurry of feathers. The tenderness inside Patsy turned over again, and she twisted her head back to the road. The big lorry had stopped, and the nearside door was being opened.

Oh, no, what was this? Should she run now, or take a chance? She needed a lift real bad.

See first, she decided. See his face.

'You after a lift?'

Patsy stared into the grey eyes. 'Yeah....'

'Well, come on, then. Look snappy, the road's narrow here.'

With no more hesitation, Patsy ran over to the cab and climbed up into the high seat next to the driver.

'Going far?' the woman asked, looking into her off-side wing mirror.

'Margate.' At that moment Patsy couldn't be sure whether she'd think that was far or not.

'You're lucky. So am I.' With precise movements of the column gear-stalk the woman pulled the lorry away, and it picked up sufficient speed to keep its place in the moving line.

Surreptitiously Patsy's eyes shifted round. The cab was comfortable and modern, and miles above the road. It gave a sort of feeling of command, of confidence. And it was all so different to what she'd expected to be in. No one would give her a second look, up here with the woman. Patsy slid back in her seat. Thank God. She was on the final bit at last. Right from the start, though, it seemed strange that nothing was being said. She'd imagined that most drivers giving lifts would start peppering you with questions. But not this one. After a few hundred metres Patsy stole some looks at her. There was something about her: a look she knew. She had a serious face, no lipstick, long, straight hair, a yellow T-shirt and jeans. About as old as Jenny, Patsy reckoned; but definitely out of another world altogether. She was sitting back in her seat with her eyes concentrating on the road, her arms relaxed, fully in charge and with none of the tension of the woman in the egg van. But what was it? Where had Patsy seen that look before?

Patsy looked out at the road again. Why worry? This was too much to have hoped for! A lift all the way to Margate and no questions being asked. So perhaps everything was going to work out after all. At this rate she'd be having a cup of tea with Mrs Broadley before she knew it.

'Why?'

Patsy started. Oh, well: it had seemed too good to be true. But you couldn't really blame the woman. And anyway, Patsy was ready. She had been for some time. Even in those few steps across the dewy verge she'd known what the answer to this question was going to be.

'Going down my gran's,' she said. 'No good waiting for buses today.'

There was no reaction; the woman just kept driving. As far as Patsy could tell she hadn't even looked at her since she got in.

'It's my mum's work,' she volunteered. 'She cleans for these people. This actress, and her old man. But he's been took ill a bit sudden, and my mum's helping. . . . They called her out last night. They've only got a little flat, though, and I'm in the way . . . you know . . . and my mum doesn't want to leave me on my own all day. So I'm going down my gran's at Margate. . . .'

Well, she might as well have the lot. That stupid play had come in useful after all. It had given her something to work on, anyway. Patsy looked at the driver to see how she'd taken it; but still her expression hadn't changed.

There was another kilometre of silence in the cab, round an island and along a straight stretch of the Thanet Way.

'Who's the actress?'

Oh. Well, that was easy, too. No one could shake a well worked-out story like the play. 'Patricia Lamont,' Patsy said. 'Have you ever heard of her?'

But there was no reply, just another question instead. 'And who's her husband?'

'Er, Gerald. He's theatrical and all. . . .'

Still no change in the driver's expression. She flicked the indicators on and off and negotiated another busy roundabout.

Patsy relaxed again; she was more than ready for anything the woman wanted to ask: her mother's name, her own name, her gran's name and address. She'd got it all off.

'And now what about the truth?'

What? The words had fallen softly into the cab like a pellet of poisonous gas. Patsy stared at the woman, eyes like marbles; and she almost had to tell herself to shut her gawping mouth. Against her will, she swallowed. The woman turned to look at her, a second of knowing in her eyes, before going back to the road again.

'Dunno what you mean. That is the truth.' Patsy managed to make herself sound really outraged.

But the woman's voice kept the same matter-of-fact tone. 'Patricia Lamont and her husband Gerald also happen to have a cleaner with a daughter—in a film called, what was it, *Happy Release*? The one on television the other night. . . .'

Now Patsy's mouth was a thin, pursed line. Oh, no! Stupid lot, picking a play that had just been on the telly! No wonder no one turned up, hardly. No wonder she couldn't fool this woman.

'Were you going to say your name was . . . Tracey, was it?'

Patsy nodded now. There wasn't much point in lying any more.

'So who are you running away from?'

The lorry hadn't slackened pace, and the woman wasn't making any suspicious moves, like turning off to a police station; her eyes didn't look as if she was on the look-out for a police car. In fact, she could have been asking about the weather.

Patsy sat there a long time, making up her mind. She wasn't

daft, this woman: she spoke like a teacher: but at the same time she definitely didn't seem the sort who'd have to go and report everything to someone in authority. She seemed pretty straight, not like one of those interfering do-gooders in a family car. . . .

Gently, a bit at a time, Patsy told her. First of all she told her about the boat, but telling it as if Jenny had been an old friend who'd invited her along on this dream trip; then gradually, as Patsy felt a certain sympathy in the way the woman nodded at the different descriptions of her own feelings, she brought Eddie Green into it: and with him, inevitably, the smacks. Slowly, it all came out about the old days in Margate; until, almost without realizing, and after lots of understanding 'ya's', all at once Patsy found she was telling her everything: the reason for the smacks, those let-down dreams, the wet beds—and to her own surprise, something she had never realized until she said it all like this, the exposure of her own deep feeling of disappointment, of betrayal, at her mother for ever starting again with another family. And now for the first time she could see that in a way it wasn't so much Eddie Green she was trying to leave behind, as Sylvia Bligh.

The drone of the cab was filled with the quiet sound of Patsy's voice, and Patsy's head with this new understanding of her own actions; till eventually there was no more to tell. And then, almost exhausted, it was over: and Patsy found a hard lump in her throat, a sort of indigestion feeling. But better. She felt a million times better for telling it all to someone. There was a long silence, until she added, finally, 'A friend of mine knows. This fat kid. But he don't know nothing about the . . . you know. . . .'

Again, a lot of road went under Patsy's feet before the woman spoke. Then in the middle of a tricky right turn she said something very softly.

'Just don't you be stupid, that's all. Don't do anything in a rush. Ever. Always hang on till you're sure. You don't want to do what some do when they're unhappy at home—run off to join the army, or something, just to get away. Or shack up with someone just because he's nice one night. That won't solve your problems, believe me. . . .' Now Patsy was staring her eyes out at the driver. She'd never been talked to like this before: not by someone who sounded as if she knew what she was talking about. 'Remember, you only ever want to do things for their own sake. . . .'

The first coach of the day suddenly occupied the woman as it cut in aggressively, its driver smiling. She let it have its way.

'Now, you go to your old lady's if you like. She sounds all right. But if you can't, hold on where you are. *Be sure*. And you'll see, things'll change before you think they will. . . .'

Patsy might have nodded. Or she might not. Just then she couldn't tell between what she was doing and what she was only thinking she was doing.

'And you've got a bit of go. That helps, too.'

Again, the driver's eyes were concentrating hard on the road: and at that moment, near the end of the ride, Patsy knew where she'd seen that concentrated look before. The man in the creek; the funny bloke; he'd had it, looking at the flower she'd given him. But what a difference. He'd only had it for a moment, and then it had gone when he'd been distracted by Kenny in the water. This woman had it all the time, that intense look of giving all of her attention to what she was doing; as if she'd never waste it on things that didn't matter. Unlike the man, she could choose where she gave her concentration, and she was giving it fiercely to her job, with a real look of purpose. Perhaps that was the answer, then, Patsy thought—having that purpose. Whether you were collecting old iron, or this woman driving a big lorry . . . or herself, getting back to Mrs Broadley.

Then perhaps she was getting it right. . . . Even more now, in a way she'd never felt on the boat even, Patsy felt pleased to have just been with her. . . .

They were driving past bungalows now: the outskirts of Margate. A big hoarding for 'Dreamland' slid by on the left, and posters for a seaside show were standing up all over the place. Now Patsy knew they were nearly there. She'd thought she'd have shouted her head off at this moment: but what the woman had said had somehow made her feel good enough already. It wasn't necessary. Being here didn't seem such a big step up any more.

'Where do you want dropping? Anywhere suits me: I'm going through to the cash-and-carry.'

'On the front, please. It's not far, I know my way....'

Margate stretched further than Patsy remembered; it seemed to take ages to get into the centre, the part Patsy knew best. But eventually they were there; and Patsy saw the familiar sight of the sandy beaches on her left and 'Dreamland' pleasure park on her right. She had often wondered how she'd feel at seeing it all again. And now she knew. A bit let-down. She remembered it sunnier than this.

There were no more questions asked; there was no more making sure. Patsy had told the driver what she wanted, and she was getting it. Now she was on her own. She had the feeling she could have said she was going to jump off the top of the 'Big Dipper', and the woman wouldn't have interfered any more. She'd said her piece—but all the decisions were Patsy's.

'Here you are, then. Good luck.'

'Thank you very much.' Patsy waved up at the cab. 'See you....'

With another loud hiss the lorry pulled away, and Patsy was left to face across the road towards the town.

It was still early, but the first arrivals of the Bank Holiday were there, shaking the shutters for their cups of tea. Patsy was looking above them, though, at the long line of sea-front buildings. Where she was going was just up behind those. Not far. A few minutes at the most. She waited for an empty open-topped bus to pass and she ran swiftly across Marine Terrace, disappearing into the side-streets that she knew so well.

The car was an old 1800, wide as a bus and finished off like something posh from a bygone age. Kenny found that there was no need to squeeze into it; you got in easily and sat in the back like a colonel.

Eddie Green got in next to him, instead of sitting up in the front with the man from the boat. That was a surprise.

The man swung round in his seat and held his hand out into the back. 'My name's Joe, Mr Green,' he said. 'Joe Miller.'

Eddie Green shook the hand readily enough. ''Ow do,' he said. But he didn't give his own first name in exchange. And Kenny was still ignored.

'I've got the car for a couple of hours. This won't take us long, though. . . .'

'No.'

'Just pick up some petrol on the way, that's all.'

'Please yourself.'

'Right. Off we go, then.'

Joe Miller revved hard and took the car away fast, up the nearest side-street, away from the harbour. Kenny sat back. Well, it did make a change, he thought, after all the walking and the slow buses. But it was going to bring things to a head very quickly now, that was the trouble.

They hadn't gone far, though, when Joe began to slow slightly, staring out hard on his right-hand side. Kenny eased himself round in his seat to see what it was. Had he spotted her? Was she there? But there was no one to be seen; just a low building with a sign painted on it; something to do with a theatre. . . .

'That's where it was,' Joe said: but neither in the back had anything to say to that, and he began to pick up speed again.

Joe handled the car well, up the empty streets, across intersections, and soon the green indicator was clinking for a left turn into the busy coast road. With a spurt, he got them

into the uniformly moving stream, and the car settled to the agreed cruising speed.

'Keep your eyes skinned!' Eddie Green told Kenny. 'Like as not she'll be walking along on your side.'

Kenny made a show of doing what he was told; but he couldn't be blamed if he somehow missed her, could he? Eddie Green's words brought the most reaction from Joe Miller. He looked pointedly in the mirror. Noisily, he cleared his throat. 'Look, Mr Green, there is something you ought to know.' He swung his head round to look directly into Eddie Green's eyes—and quickly back to the road again.

'Yeah?' Eddie Green was looking out on the right, pre-occupied. Kenny could see that he certainly wouldn't lean forward.

'About Patsy. You ought to know. . . .' He scratched his neck: and a sudden tingling played on the surface of Kenny's skin. *Was she all right?* 'You ought to know, I did guess about her, Mr Green. I had a sort of an idea. . . . Not right off, mind. It's hard to say when. But I did guess she'd run away, in spite of the note. And I told her, too . . . I want you to know that. Before Patsy tells you I knew, I want to get it in the open. . . .'

Eddie Green sat frowning, staring at the back of Joe's neck. Joe's anxious eyes flickered in the mirror. And Kenny sank back as far as he could in his seat. Was there going to be a punch-up after all? His fingers found the handgrip in the door, his knuckles pressing white.

'Oh, yeah?'

'Well, I suppose it could seem strange that I never did anything about it: didn't tell the police, for instance. . . .'

'Yeah; I s'pose it could. . . .'

'And of course, I should have. I can see that now. But. . . .' he dropped his voice almost to inaudibility. 'Oh, it's a long story. Goes back a long way. . . .' He checked in the mirror again; but not for following vehicles. 'Let's just say I had my reasons. . . .' The driving part of him overtook a lorry up an incline, but the rest seemed years away. 'It was good, having a bright little thing around. And . . . well, I was stupid, but I thought . . . one more day. . . .'

Eddie Green's eyes had lost their sharpness now. He was sitting back, looking out of his side window just as he'd stared out of the train when they'd first begun. Kenny turned back to his own side of the road. Life was full of these surprises, he thought. And it had all changed such a lot over the past two days. At first he'd been frightened of the man, and he'd hated him, walking round in his circles and snapping at the rails; but then Eddie Green had really looked after him, and there'd been that great time, living rough, with all the talk about jumping across the green towers and everything; and today Kenny was ending up feeling sorry for him, sitting hunched up now like a man in a hearse. Heavy-handed or not, it must come hard when everyone was showing you up. . . .

The car had stopped: and Kenny came to. They were in a petrol station, and Joe was getting out. He slammed the door, leaving the two of them alone in the back, rocking in their seats as he undid the petrol cap and shoved the nozzle in.

Eddie Green lit a cigarette, filling the car with smoke. Somewhere beneath Kenny the petrol sluiced in. He became aware of it at the same time as his wandering eye found the 'No Smoking' sign on the pump. But the way he felt right now it wasn't worth a second thought. Whatever had been there between them for a bit, him and Eddie Green, was gone now; and he was Kenny Granger again, on his own; 'Fatso' from Deptford. Quietly in his seat he started to flex his muscles.

'Why, Kenny?' Eddie Green had twisted towards him, and his eyes were narrowed with a real look of wanting to know. 'Now, you're a mate of 'ers. You know 'er secrets. You tell me why she went and took that risk. She could've been killed with a load of nutters like that. . . .'

Kenny stared back at him. Again, just the same as with his mum, he felt that he was the man, with the grown-up the kid. God, didn't he know, really? The rest of the world could see, but still not Patsy's father. What did you say to that, then? How the hell could you give an honest answer? Well, a big shrug and 'Search me!' could be the obvious way. But as Kenny looked into those shrewd eyes he realized there was no way he could give him that. This bloke would see right through a pretence of that sort, especially from him. They'd got to know each other a bit too well in the past couple of days....

Of course Kenny knew. *But how could he tell him?*

Eddie Green was filling the long, sluicing wait by going on about her not understanding him; about him giving her everything she wanted, her own room, and all the rest. But Kenny wasn't listening to all that: he was thinking about Patsy herself, thoughts which, almost despite himself, were swelling like balloons inside his head. He found his pulse beating faster, his throat starting to hurt, and his lungs suddenly feeling empty. He knew what it was. Come hell or high water he was about to tell Eddie Green the truth. It was inevitable. It had come to that. He couldn't stop himself now if he wanted to.

He interrupted the man. It was no good waiting. It had to come out now or he could never face Patsy again. He had to get it over with. He jumped in on Eddie Green's words, and in a thin, nervous, voice he told him.

'Well, I'll tell you why I reckon she's done it if you like.... She's done it because she's just the same as you was....'

Eddie Green had shut his mouth and he was staring at Kenny.

'She's done the same as you done when you was a kid. She's run off the same as you did, from your old man. She's done the same thing ....' Kenny wasn't putting it very well; but he knew what he wanted to say; because he knew that the three of them, Eddie Green, him, and Patsy were all the same. 'Like when you went swimming when it was dangerous. Like when you ran across the railway line; and when you jumped across them big towers. When you didn't care what happened.

168

I reckon that's what she's done. The same....'

Eddie Green was frowning now. 'No, you're out of order there,' he said quickly. 'My old man was....' He put on a hard, spiteful face. And Kenny knew that everyone but Eddie Green would have seen it: the similarity. All right, so perhaps Patsy was doing it to get away for good: but that was only because she thought she could. Without her Mrs Broadley to think about, God knew what she'd have been doing.

'So that's what you reckon, is it? Good God Almighty....' Eddie Green puffed energetically at his cigarette, like someone trying hard to lay a smoke-screen. 'Good God Almighty,' he repeated.

Joe Miller opened the driver's door and sucked out some of the smoke. 'Sorry,' he said. 'But I promised I'd tank it up. Won't take us long now.' He went to sit in, but he stopped half-way and twisted round to face the quiet Eddie Green. 'I ... er ... I hope you understand, Mr Green, what I was telling you about.'

He was still scared, that was obvious. He was scared of Eddie Green the same way as Patsy was.

This time Eddie Green didn't ignore what Joe was saying. 'Forget it.' He threw his stub-end out of the window. 'Just don't say no more about it. I've 'ad enough 'ome truths for today, thank you very much.'

Joe coughed. 'Anyway, let's find her, eh? What was the address?' He rocked the car again as he bounced relieved into his seat.

'Twenty-eight Keats Road. Up behind "Dreamland". That's where she'll be....'

Again the car smoothly picked up speed. Kenny rested his head back, feeling exhausted. There was no alternative now for any of them but to go to the address and see this out. Inside, though, he was groaning; and the sight of the first big splatters of rain on the windscreen seemed to say it all for him at the moment.

'Would you believe it. Bloody rain!' Joe found the wipers and the screen wash.

'Well, it had to change,' said Eddie Green, quietly. 'It always does. . . .'

13

Patsy ran the familiar streets in the wet, her dress clinging like thin plastic, her splashed legs moving as if they were oiled. But although the weather had broken—bursting like a balloon of water a few moments before, everything falling at once—it hadn't affected her spirits. Back in Deptford it would have mattered: bad weather kept you imprisoned in the flat. Now, wet or fine, it would all be the same in a bit, over a cup of tea with Mrs Broadley in Keats Road.

All along Patsy had put off thinking about this meeting. She'd thought quite a bit about what would happen later on: the things they'd do together, the outings in the sun, and the quiet evenings on their own: but she'd found this first meeting hard to work out in her mind, and she'd deliberately left it as a blur, something which would all happen somehow, all come right, like first days in a new class. She knew she'd be recognized with a big, special smile, and she'd be hugged till she couldn't breathe, and then they'd both cry, and there'd be a very upset ten minutes while she told Mrs Broadley all her troubles. But quite what she'd say, and what Mrs Broadley would do at first, was the awkward bit which was hard to imagine.

So Patsy was running hard to get through the awkward bit as quickly as she could, through to the nice times she knew were on the other side.

This road leading up to Mrs Broadley's turning was just the same as if she'd never been away. Even in the rain, running, she could remember that same house where they never cut the hedge; and that same little wall made with sea-shells. That was hopeful she thought; after her first fresh look at Margate from the lorry this made her feel good, knowing it was all still there really, just the way she remembered it. She ran on. Not much further now.

There had been one big fear, but she hadn't ever let herself think about it; anyway, not for any longer than it took to turn her mind to something else. Now it seemed safe enough to bring it out for a second or so. Reassured by every familiar sight along the street, she ran over her secret dread: her fear that all this would be knocked down, and in its place big blocks of flats with muddy grass and puddles of car oil, like in Deptford. Or shops. The dread that the whole place would be changed, with everything cleared, houses pulled down and everybody gone away. That was what she'd dreaded. But with every step she took Patsy could see that it was all exactly the same as it used to be. She even remembered the pattern of cracks on a particular paving stone, the spider slab she'd jumped over every day. It all came back to her now: a dream coming true.

Without slackening speed she turned the last corner. Boldly, she looked up. Keats Road. Just the same. Just like in the song, it was all right now.

Number twenty-eight. Down here on the right, in the middle of the row. She screwed her eyes and hardly dared to look. Excitement and the running thumped inside her chest. Twenty-four, twenty-six, and—God, where had her breath gone?—number twenty-eight. She stopped and drew wet air into her burning lungs. There it was! The same oval number on the door; the same crinkly glass; the same net curtains at the window.

Patsy had never felt so excited in all her life. Here she was at last. Here was the house. Here was her Mrs Broadley, probably out in the back addition, washing her bits, or cooking scones, singing to the radio like she'd always done. She'd made it. She was back where she really wanted to be.

She just about had enough breath now. She could talk.

Cautiously, she walked up the short path, and with only a second's hesitation, she pressed on the same white bell-push that she'd never been able to reach before. And there was the same old crackling ring.

Patsy's stomach turned over with anticipation.

A noise. Definitely someone coming. A vague outline through the crinkly glass. A hand reaching for the lock. The door opening.

'Yes?'

Oh, God, no! Not after all that! The wrong house! It had looked the same, but it was definitely the wrong one. She must have made a mistake with the number, because this was a man, in his vest.

'Sorry ... I got the wrong place. I'm looking for Mrs Broadley's house....' She turned away. Try two doors further along. What must have happened was, she'd passed this house a lot as a kid, and she'd thought she recognized it as the one. Stupid thing to do; but it had been a couple of years....

'No, hold on, girlie....'

The man was leaning back inside, keeping the door open with his foot. Patsy could see up the hall now.

And at that instant the wishing fell out of her dreams; the bottom out of her world. This was it. There was that picture of Mary on the wall: just the same as she remembered it. She'd looked at that face often enough to know. And that looking-glass.... The faintest hope tried to tell her the man might have come from upstairs, their old flat, but his manner had told her that wasn't so. She knew she didn't need to hear what was going on between the man and someone in the back.

'Bridie, what was the old girl's name, for God's sake?'

'Eh?'

'The old lady who was here. I'll be damned if I can remember her name....'

'Who? Who we had it from?' A young woman with long,

auburn hair came from the back room to stand sideways in the hall, staring at Patsy. 'Mrs Broadley. Why?'

'This little girlie here's asking after her....'

'Oh.' The woman looked suspiciously at Patsy, as if she'd come to reclaim the house. 'You'd better tell your mum to ask at the Town Hall, love. They'd know where they took her. But tell your mum she must have died in the end, because we bought it after, lock, stock and barrel. It all belongs to us now. Can you explain all that?'

The man began to shut the door against the encroaching rain. 'All right, dear? Bye-bye.' He closed it.

Patsy stood in the front garden like a fountain-figure, her mouth open as if she'd been caught in protest by her sculptor, her arms still, and dripping by her sides; her eyes closed against the world; and inside, her heart and spirit suddenly turned to stone.

She couldn't grasp it. Dead? That was impossible. Mrs Broadley couldn't be dead: she was an alive person. She wasn't nearly old enough to die from being ill. She was a young old lady. Dissolving images appeared inside Patsy's head, the first thoughts of her baffled grief remembered moments of Mrs Broadley—telling her little secrets, doing the small garden, winning an argument with a bus conductor, talking and laughing with Patsy's mum as if they were both eighteen. All that life couldn't suddenly be gone. It was unbelievable.

And devastating. Patsy had no plans for this. She knew she'd have followed and found her in a new block of flats, even in a new town. But *dead*? It was a blanked off end, like the wall at the bottom of River Street. There couldn't be any following her beyond that.

It was the finish. There was nothing left for Patsy any more, nowhere to go, just a hugh emptiness. She felt sick, and her next indrawn breath trembled in her chest, the first choke of tears. Now there was no point in anything; not any more. It was all over: all the pictures she'd had in her head up on the roof of the school: all the hassle of running away: all those fears and worries had been for nothing. She might as well just fall down on the ground right here and let the cold rain kill her. . . .

A quiet car swished in the gutter. It wasn't until the second door slammed that Patsy turned. For just a split second she thought it could be Mrs Broadley, getting out of the welfare's car and coming over to tell Patsy it had all been a stupid mistake: a sort of second chance. Or it could have been a waking up from another nasty dream. Patsy rubbed her eyes with her finger tips, and saw more clearly through the railings.

Eddie Green! And Joe! Fear, like wet static, flashed through her body. Both of them were standing there staring. And they had Kenny Granger sitting up in the back of the car.

Kenny Granger? And these other two together? Her mind couldn't make sense of it. Unless it *was* one of those terrible dreams, when all sorts of weird things got linked up with one another. Please God she'd wake in a minute, and find it was just the usual. . . .

Hold on! Eddie Green coming towards her with his hand on the gate seemed like real life. . . . 'Patsy! Patsy!' he was saying. His voice was very clear, somehow. Quiet, but clear. And its reality acted to bring Patsy out of her shock. No, this was no terrible dream, she told herself. This was real! She could still feel herself really worn out from running here, and she was really wet from all the rain. It was lounging about in the sunshine on that boat that had been the dream; acting all that make-believe rubbish on a stage: not this. This was the real life. And this was the real Eddie Green coming to get her back!

Like a cat cornered in its own yard, she shot to a familiar route of escape. There was a small gate which some part of her brain remembered being in the side fence dividing this house from next door: the old neighbour's easy way in to Mrs Broadley. It was still there. Before Eddie Green could realize it, she was half-way across next door's front and out through the open gap into the street.

Head down in the rain, her speed fuelled by fear and by panic, she ran from him as she had never run in all her life before. Everything she had ever wanted to get away from stood behind her in the street, and every last ounce of her energy was going to keep her a safe distance away.

Caught by surprise, Eddie Green's reaction seemed slow. He made a move after her, but it wasn't the catch-you-and-kill-you determined grab he'd have made in the flats at Deptford. It was more of a defeated lunge. His short run quickly petered out, and he beckoned to Joe to follow with the car, while he walked and trotted behind, just fast enough to keep Patsy in sight. To Kenny, in the back, it looked like one of the teachers going after a kid who's lost his temper; someone who for reasons of his own was wanting to play it cool.

The energy Patsy found was the final effort of the hunted animal: the energy that can sustain both sprint and stamina for a remarkable distance, but which gambles on not needing to have the strength to turn and fight in the end. Stumbling and slipping, she ran back the way she had come, along the empty side-street pavements until she found herself on the front once more. Quick glances back through the rain had shown her Eddie Green still coming, and that maroon car cruising. But she couldn't out-run them on the streets, she knew that; so what else could she do? It wasn't easy to think, gasping for the next burning breath, chest tight to bursting point, legs threatening to give up and leave her shattered on the hard shine of the pavement: there wasn't much planning left in her any more.

But hold on, she coaxed herself, there was one place she knew about: there was just a slim chance she could lose herself for a bit, long enough to sort out the last tatters of everything in her mind.

The sky growled, and drove the last of the hurrying trippers off the wide pavement into the swollen bingo parlours. Patsy ran past them, to amplified voices chanting

176

after her: 'Unlucky for some, thirteen'; 'On its own, number one'.

She looked back. Eddie Green was still coming: he'd turned the corner and he must be able to see her out on her own in the rain. She ran on, urging herself to the place; where the car couldn't follow her, which opened out inside with enough room for her to get herself lost. 'Dreamland'. She knew the place, everyone did; and there'd be crowds in there in this rain. Even if it had to be in one of the crowded ladies' lavs, she was sure she could lose him in 'Dreamland'.

It was a final effort. Choking sick with the run, with the band round her chest twisted as tight as the knot round her head, she swayed in through the wide entrance. It was killing her now, but thank God, she was right: there were crowds of people under there in the dry.

Patsy twisted through them, bashing into slow movers, stumbling over clumsy kids, while the ring and rattle of the machines, the electric explosions of direct hits, the silver cascade and hoarse shouts of a pay-out, sounded like a nightmare in her ears. Coloured lights flashed in her face and neon arrows shot their stupid messages into the air. Mirrors threw her back at herself, now a tall, skinny thing in wet pink, now a midget-legged creature scurrying under a fat nylon balloon.

She remembered all this. It didn't seem any time at all since she'd been here before; but she'd been strolling through the crowds, then, holding tight to Mrs Broadley's hand. Steered, and protected; safe, like all these other kids with their mums and dads.

She looked around between the barricading stomachs and chests. She couldn't see him; which meant he couldn't see her. At least that had worked, for the minute. But now she found she couldn't stop. Now that it was the time and the place she hadn't got the confidence to stop and lose herself here. It was all too confusing on her own. Only space and distance were the answer now. Go on and through, she told herself, get out into the huge amusement park at the back: keep on running, and find a place to think with plenty of space all around. Feel safe. Get out of this screaming nightmare.

In the pouring rain it was all empty outside: and when she saw it again the wide open space stopped her, like a negative magnetic field. Stupid! What the hell had she been thinking? She couldn't go out there; not right out in the middle. With no one there she'd be seen a mile away. Frantically, she looked to right and left. Round the edges was the only way, over there where all the rifle shooting and tin-can throwing went on. But where after that? The dodgems were going, and there were people still screaming down the 'Big Dipper', even in the rain. But she'd be seen on them, just as easy. Get in the 'Tunnel of Love', or the 'Haunted House'—that'd be the answer. You could lose yourself in them, if you had the money to get in. But you could stop and think in a place like that. . . .

She was just about all in. Half-walking, half-running, she skirted the ranges.

'Come on, miss, try your luck. Win yourself something nice.'

Every breath was a killing pain now. What about over there? Yes, she'd just get round behind the water-chute, where she could see things. From there she could see who came out of the covered part to look for her in the open. Then she could think. But she must have a quick breather first. She bent double and heaved her lungs out at the ground. She spat. Like a cross-country runner with the stitch she held her sides and straightened to look over her shoulder. No, nobody coming yet. He was still lost in the crowds inside. Time to get over there where she wanted. . . .

The hand on her shoulder was like the sudden feel of death. Patsy knew who it was. He'd come through some short cut to get in front of her. She'd forgotten he used to work here.

' 'Ere, Patsy. . . .' Eddie Green was frowning.

Patsy screamed. She screeched to the sky, and she kicked at his legs. Her flailing fists hit the hardness of his body. A rifle-

178

range woman shouted at him. Patsy twisted at his grip and her wet shoulder slipped from under him.

'Get off!' she cried.

She ran. She didn't know where. She just ran, without looking back. He'd get her any second; any second now and she'd feel that hand on her shoulder again, or a smack round the head to send her sprawling over in the wet.

But she wasn't giving in. Straight across the space she ran, surprised with every step that there was no hand yet. Someone might have stopped him, the pounding said, someone who thought he was up to no good. But he'd come, in the end he'd come....

Over there! She saw a white fence, with its gate open. The 'Big Slide'. And no one on it in the rain. A sign saying 'Closed'. Stuff that! she told herself. Bash through the gate and up them wooden stairs. Run! Stupid little steps she was having to take. Legs going fifty to the dozen, killing her. Up, and up; to the top. Yeah, get up to the top: and turn round: and scream and shout at him in front of all the people. Let them all know....

'Hey, you! Come back down. We're closed.'

Patsy gave the very last of everything to get to the top, to heave her lungs at the head of a dipping lane and see the rain running down in shallow tides back to the bottom, and Eddie Green.

There he was; she could see him, talking to the man who ran it, pointing up at her.

Patsy sucked in rain like wet fire. She was bent again, over the safety rail; and she was finished. This was it: she knew it. Whether Eddie Green came up or not, there was only one way back from here. She heaved again, and coughed. She pressed her legs against an upright to make them hold her up. Just staying conscious now was so painful that she was ready to let everything go.

She'd failed. She'd been run to a halt; and she hadn't even found herself the time to think. As for shouting at Eddie

Green, she hadn't got the breath to keep herself in oxygen. . . .

Behind her, a 'Big Dipper' rumbled round an aerial bend. If she'd been more alert it would have startled her. Slowly, she lifted her head to watch it go by. There were people in it, just one or two; and they'd waved at her; or pointed. She could almost have touched them.

She put her head down again; and raised it in the same movement as a wild possibility suddenly came into her head. Really wild; but just possible. . . . The 'Big Dipper' track. It was no more than two metres away. Well, it could be done, couldn't it? She could get across. There was an alternative to going back down to him, after all. . . .

Now Patsy was standing up. She looked down at the entrance to the slide. A small crowd had gathered there; but no one was making any move to come up the steps and get her. Not yet. They were all too busy talking. She squinted through the glaze of rain. Yes. She thought so. Joe was down there now: and Kenny. Kenny, the fat creep. . . . And Jenny! She was there, too. She must have been following, met up with the others on the front.

But Patsy's attention quickly went back to the gap behind her. It wasn't so crazy, she thought. If she could get on to that 'Big Dipper', she could run back along that track, go down that dip, and get on to that wall over there that separated 'Dreamland' from the outside. She'd be away then. It'd take Eddie Green ages to get round there the proper way.

Patsy measured it with her eyes. It was a good jump. But if she gave her legs a minute, and then got up on the railing, and balanced, and really took off, well. . . . She should do it. With a bit of luck. . . .

And if she couldn't? Patsy looked down at the ground. It was a long way to fall. It'd kill her.

She tasted something strange in her mouth; something bitter. Well, she suddenly thought, so what if it did? That'd show Eddie Green. And her mum. That'd show them all. It'd show everyone what life was worth to her now: what she felt like. Now Mrs Broadley was dead, what was there for her? She looked down at the crowd again, sort of willing her message to Eddie Green. Yeah, and what about the rest of the people she knew? There was that Joe down there: well, there was no trusting people like him. And Kenny. Her only real mate, she'd thought, and he'd been the one to lead them to her. No, there was nothing for her if she did get out of the park. It was just about worth the one try, an outside chance: and if it failed it wouldn't matter to anyone in the world. . . .

She turned her back on them all. They could start coming now, and they'd never get up here in time to stop her. She looked out over the sea. The grey, unbroken sky hung low, like a final curtain; and on the water the white tops were flickering on the waves, like little lights. She stared at it all, her eyes unfocussed. She caught on a breath. It was funny, she thought, but where she was standing was about the height of the school roof: and there was all that same water down there. Who'd ever have reckoned those stupid dreams would end like this?

All right! She was definitely going to make a jump for it. She'd show the whole lot of them the chance she was prepared to take: let them see just the way things were for her.

But first, she took a last look back; not down at the people below this time, but out across the town of Margate. Her place, where she'd come from. From up here she could see past Mrs Broadley's road to the thin strip of the Thanet Way, on the horizon. She could see all the cars and coaches crawling to the seaside, looking like Jason's Matchbox toys. And she could see lorries, one or two; and one big one going back the other way. People still carrying on, like that woman.

The edge of her sad, nostalgic look suddenly hardened. Yeah, that woman. She'd forgotten her in all the panic. That driver. Funny she should forget her because she'd liked her, the way she hadn't interfered in things: kept herself to just giving a bit of advice. Patsy's sharp eyes followed the lorry till it was no more than a flaw on her retina. They were a lot like each other, from the way she'd talked, her and that woman. She'd had a rough time, too. And she'd done the same as Patsy's mum, made a big mistake and gone off with some man who'd been nice one night, like Eddie Green. That was obvious from what she'd said. Yes, she knew all about men like Eddie Green. Patsy blinked in the rain. Not that she could picture it, Eddie Green being nice. Hands that hit as hard as his couldn't stroke as well, could they?

Patsy shifted her feet and turned to look down at him. He was making for the little gate. But she could easy jump before he got there. When she was ready. Don't do nothing in a rush.

She'd said that, too, hadn't she? Hang on till you're sure.

Patsy looked at the 'Big Dipper' again. But now she could hear him coming up; coming slowly, she could tell by the creaks. She turned her attention back. Yes, he was on his way; but he wasn't on his own. Jenny was there, too. Jenny was coming up with him, a step behind, and trying to smile. But Patsy gave them only part of her attention. Like she'd felt when she'd first done the play, she could think on two levels at once. She was aware of them, and what they were doing now; and she was aware of herself, of Patsy Bligh, and of other times and places. . . .

'Come on, lovey, we understand.' They had stopped short, and Jenny was doing the talking, blinking at her through the rain. 'Come on down. You mustn't worry so much about things, sweetheart. There are some things you mustn't let get you down. . . .' She was looking hard with her eyes and trying to smile with her mouth, obviously searching desperately for the right things to say to get Patsy's attention. 'Look, lovey, you're not the only one, you know. Like that bed business. Millions do it. And it gets better, you know. You grow out of things, lots of us have. They're only childhood problems. . . .'

Patsy stared at her now, all her attention was there, all on the one level.

'Honestly, millions do, lovey....'

Patsy swallowed. Her? Jenny—the dream girl on the boat, all posh and beautiful the first time she'd seen her, like an advert on the telly—did she used to have those funny dreams? Had she followed her all the way from Steeple Stones to tell her this?

'We all think we're the only ones, lovey. So we don't know. But they come to an end, almost before you know it. You see, sweetheart....' She was trying to smile some confidence at her, just as she had after the play. And Eddie Green was standing there, listening, frowning a bit as he looked at Jenny.

'I should have said, shouldn't I—about the bed business? We could have talked about it. But that's me! I knew, when you wouldn't have a drink in the evening, when you made those last-minute visits to the loo. I knew enough to put a sheet of plastic on your bunk; and still I didn't say anything. I'm stupid, like that....'

Patsy could only stare. The world was spinning round, turning everything upside-down. Everything was such a muddle. It was too late, telling her all this now. Why couldn't someone have said these things before? It was too late to be finding all these other people around: Mrs Broadley wasn't, that was what was hitting her the hardest of all.

'Things will be all right, won't they?' Jenny had turned to Eddie Green: and he was nodding his head, almost. And now Patsy stared at him.

'Come on, Patsy,' he said. 'We'll 'ave a talk about it, with your mum. She's worried out of her mind.'

Was there any trusting him? Patsy was still trying desperately to sort things out in her head. Was this just some show he was putting on while he was there with Jenny. Patsy took a quick look at the distance across the gap again. It seemed a bit further now. She glanced down—straight down, at the ground. And that was a hell of a long way. . . .

'Patsy! Come on, there ain't no need for that. You ain't got nothing to prove by jumping nowhere. . . .'

What was that? Patsy swung back to look at him. How did Eddie Green know what she was thinking. Jumping across had been in *her* mind, not in his.

She went on staring at him; shocked at what he'd said, and measuring how far away he was. And as she stared, to surprise and muddle her more, he turned and began going slowly back, down the steps, guiding Jenny with him. What had come over him? Patsy thought. The Eddie Green she was used to would have tried to yank her down, Jenny or not, just to save his face with everyone.

No. Now she knew. It's all down to you, he was saying. Make your own mind up. She looked all round, at the wide open space of 'Dreamland', and at the two different figures retreating beneath her. Oh, God, it was all such a big muddle now. She'd decided to run off: and it had all gone wrong. Then she was going to show everyone what she thought of him in that last chance of a jump across: and now he was telling her to go ahead if she felt she had to, if she was that unhappy. Do it, he was saying; or come back down and go home.

She took in a deep breath of Margate air and fresh rain. Well, it took time to make your mind up, she thought. There were all the different things you had to think about, the different reasons you had for doing them: running off, or lying about on boats, or making believe . . . different reasons for showing everyone up or hanging on.

But of them all, the reasons, the voices she heard the loudest—the most insistent at that moment—were those of Jenny and the lorry driver. Things get better before you know it, Jenny had said: and Jenny had known; had tried to say it at the play. And don't do nothing in a rush, she'd been told in the cab. Apart from all that everything was muddle and failure; the muddle of all the rights and wrongs of doing this

184

and doing that; and the failure of never meeting up with Mrs Broadley. . . .

Patsy stood, stock still; and suddenly, without really making any final decision, that was as far as she wanted it all to go. She didn't know what was right. She couldn't be sure that she knew anything any more. Everything was too much for her now. Patsy hadn't a decision left in her. She lowered her head, and quietly, she began to cry. Like someone giving in under enormous pressure, she slowly folded up, crouching down at the top of the slope, the picture of a defeated refugee when a war has passed; and she cried it all out till there were no more tears to come; till she felt empty of everything inside.

And when the sound of it had stopped, she knew that still there was no one near. Eddie Green had made everyone leave her alone; and he was waiting quietly below. There was no more shouting from anywhere: no more persuasion, not from them, not from anywhere inside her head.

Deliberately, steadying herself on the rail, she stood up and began to take the slow way back to the bottom; step by step, staring all the time at her feet. And then she got to him, and she stopped; and still she wouldn't look up.

His hand took hers, smoother than her mother's, and it firmly guided her away. Without a word he walked her back through the crowds and the pouring rain to a place under cover: a café where they could sit, and get a cup of tea; and wait for Kenny Granger to find them.